MW00883709

# THE BOOKSELLER AND THE EARL

THE MERRY MISFITS OF BATH ~ BOOK ONE

CALLIE HUTTON

Author's website: http://calliehutton.com/

Cover design by Maria Connor, My Author Concierge

Manufactured in the United States of America

First Edition October 2019

## ABOUT THE BOOK

Miss Addie Mallory is finished with the husband hunt. After six London Seasons as a wallflower, she convinces her parents that she should be allowed to use her dowry to buy a bookstore in Bath where she can live her life the way she wants.

Lord Grayson, Earl of Berkshire, has never gotten over his deceased wife's betrayal with his own brother. He plans to make his life all about his son, Michael, who is deaf. When Grayson's sister-in-law serves him with court papers declaring Michael incompetent with the intention of having her own son named as Grayson's rightful heir, he turns to Addie, a dyslexic bookstore owner, for help.

Addie takes a personal interest in helping the boy. However, as time passes, Grayson and Addie's joint venture to keep Michael from being declared incompetent leads to feelings and desires neither one of them expected.

Or necessarily wanted.

*To Anna, who battles dyslexia every day.*

# AUTHOR'S NOTE

Dyslexia is much more than reversing letters. At least in this enlightened age, the condition is not thought to be a lack of intelligence, as it was in previous years.

Dyslexia is a condition that affects more than the way you read. Dyslexics have a problem with directions – right, left, up, down, forward, backward. They have issues with social inter- actions and of course, a lack of self-esteem after so many fail- ures to do and see what everyone else seems to accomplish with little effort.

Well-known dyslexics are among the most accomplished people in the world. Leonardo Da Vinci, Walt Disney, Albert Einstein, John Lennon, Pablo Picasso, and Steven Spielberg are a few of many among the group.

If you would like some additional information on how a child in school deals with dyslexia, there is a very interesting and eye-opening video available on YouTube when this book was written, called "How Difficult Can This Be – The F.A.T. City Workshop."

When my daughter, who deals with this every day, was going through school, I asked every one of her teachers to watch it. They found it so informative that many passed it along to their peers. As I say, a true eye-opener.

I hope you enjoyed the story of Addie and her love of books, even though they were a struggle for her to read.

# PROLOGUE

*February 1885*
*London, England*

MISS ADELINE MALLORY ACCEPTED THE FOOTMAN'S HAND AND climbed from the carriage in front of her family's townhouse in Mayfair. Her chaperone, Mrs. Wesley, followed her down the two short steps, then up the stone pathway to the stairs leading to the gleaming white front door with the well-polished brass knocker shaped like a roaring lion.

Before she reached the top step, the door was opened by Grimsley, their ancient and much-loved butler. "Good evening, Miss Mallory. I hope you had a pleasant time at the ball."

She didn't have the heart to tell him that she had yet another entry to add to her ongoing chronicle *Adeline Leaves the House.* That was the running saga she kept in her journal, where each day she recorded the mishaps that happened to her every time she left the comfort of her home. Not that her life was full of mishaps—well, not all her life—but there were certainly enough to fill the pages of the three journals she'd kept since she had been old enough to write.

Tonight's misfortune, however, was the proverbial last straw. This Season was starting out no better than all the others. The red stain on her pale blue ball gown was a stark reminder of her clumsiness. Although she had a good reason to believe one of the girls who had hated her for years purposely jarred her elbow, making her glass of punch spill down the front.

While she still had the anger churning in her stomach, she smiled and nodded at Grimsley, then marched down the corridor to the drawing room. Precisely where she knew her parents would be sitting this time of night, mother doing her endless needlework and father reading.

Such a peaceful couple, how could they have produced such a clumsy, inept daughter? Adeline pushed away the self-pity slowly making its way into her thoughts. She'd accepted a long time ago that she was not like other girls. And at every single event for the past six years, the other girls made sure she knew it.

Shifting the material on the front of her gown to cover the red stain, she said, "Good evening, Mother. Father."

Her parents looked up from their tasks and smiled at her. The love in their eyes almost brought her to her knees. How would they receive the request she was about to make? The last thing she would ever want to do was to hurt them, but she'd made up her mind on the way home from the Everson ball, and nothing would dissuade her.

"How was your evening, my dear?" Mother patted the spot alongside her on the sofa as an invitation for Adeline to join her. Taking a deep breath, she settled next to Mother. "It was a typical ball. Nothing different."

"No special gentleman?" Father grinned.

"No. I'm afraid not." She kept a bright smile on her face, even though she was all knotted up inside and felt as if she were about to burst into tears. If she showed any sort of weakness, she would never get their permission.

Mother patted her hand. "Not to worry, dear. The right man will present himself when the time is right."

"Soon, I hope," Father mumbled as he picked up his book to continue reading.

"Arthur!" Mother chastised.

"Sorry, I didn't mean it the way it came out." He raised his book to cover his face.

"Father, I need your attention." She turned toward her mother. "Yours, as well, Mother."

Unable to sit any longer, Adeline hopped up and moved back a few spaces so she could see both of her parents clearly. It was nice to have a good view when one was about to break one's parents' hearts. "I shall not participate in another Season. I have attended my last ball."

Two pairs of blue eyes similar to her own looked up at her, Mother with a slight frown, Father with a more pronounced one. "What do you mean, dearest?" Mother said.

"I am twenty-four years old, and by most measuring sticks, a spinster." She raised her palm when both parents opened their mouths to speak. "Please let me finish. It doesn't matter that you don't think I am a spinster. The rest of the world perceives me as such."

Mother glanced over at Father, a look passing between them she'd seen many times before. It was the 'whatever is she talking about now' expression.

Before she lost her nerve, she continued. "I am aware of my shortcomings and have accepted them."

Father shifted in his chair and placed his book on the table next to him. "Now wait just a minute—"

"Please, Father. Hear me out." She needed to stay angry. If she succumbed to their defense of her, and their resistance to see her as she actually was, she would dissolve into tears, and nothing would change.

"I believe it is time for me to make my own way in the world."

Mother sucked in a deep breath and placed her hand over her mouth. "What do you mean?"

"I want to move away from London. And more than that, I want to own a bookstore."

"You want to work!?" Father came right up out of his chair. "No daughter of mine will work. And that is the end of it."

Her mother withdrew a lace-trimmed white handkerchief from the sleeve of her dress and patted her eyes. "What have we done to make you want to do this to us?"

Adeline dropped to her knees and took her mother's hand. "I am not doing anything to either of you. I love you both with my whole heart. But the life you have always planned for me is not going to happen. In six years of husband-hunting, not one gentleman has shown any interest."

"There was Mr. Abercrombie," Mother said.

Addie sat back on her heels. "Mother. The man was fifty years old with children older than me. And," she added with a smirk on her face, "he needed my dowry."

"Arthur, say something to her," Mother begged.

Father looked back and forth between her and her mother, and his face softened. "Perhaps she is right, Mildred."

"What?" The screech coming from her mother probably brought all the horses in Mayfair to an abrupt halt.

Father studied her, tapping his lips with his finger. "Maybe it is time. I know it is not the normal thing for a young lady to move from her parents' home and strike out on her own, but it might be the right thing for our daughter."

Mother moaned. "I cannot believe the two of you." She looked down at Adeline, still on the floor at her feet. "You must find a nice man. All right, maybe Mr. Abercrombie was not for you, but I shall ask among my friends. There are many sons, cousins, nephews, and friends of friends who we might introduce to you."

Adeline shook her head. "No, Mother. I am finished with the game. I don't care if I never have a husband. I don't care if I never have a child"—a slight lie there—"but I want to feel as though there is more to my life than changing clothes and attending social affairs."

Father moved to sit on the arm of the sofa and rested his hand on Mother's shoulder. "This sounds like something you've thought about for some time. What do you have in mind?"

Excited that Father would actually consider her plan, she demurely placed her hands in her lap and stared up at him. "There is a bookstore in Bath for sale."

"Bath!" Mother moaned again. "That's on the other side of the country."

Ignoring her mother's outburst, Adeline continued, "Since I will have no need for a dowry, I had hoped you would allow me to use the funds to buy the bookstore. I would get a small flat nearby and run the store." She smiled, enthused about her plans. "You know how much I love books."

"But you can't read," Mother wailed.

*Thank you, Mother.* It was always nice to hear one's faults so adequately expressed.

"I can read, Mother. It just is a bit difficult for me."

Ever since she'd picked up her first book and looked at the words, she'd had a problem. It appeared no one else saw what she saw because when she read, it all came out wrong. When her teacher told them she was lacking intelligence, her parents had removed her from school and hired a tutor.

The tutor worked with her for years. She suggested that Adeline suffered from something recently termed *word blindness,* and she would have it her whole life. All Adeline knew of the condition was everyone else could read a book in a flash, their eyes moving back and forth over the lines on the page, while she had to stumble over every word. But that never stopped her love for books.

She loved the feel of the book in her hands. She loved the smell of the ink when she opened the tome for the first time.

She loved turning the pages, smiling, as if she could read that fast. 'Twas difficult when one loved something that didn't love one back.

Just then, her elder brother, Marcus, entered the room and saw her kneeling at her mother's feet. "Paying homage to the Queen, Adeline?"

"No. I'm pleading for a change in my life."

He walked to the sideboard and poured a small glass of brandy. Tall, confident, handsome, and charming, Adeline always idolized her brother, wishing she could be more like him and less like herself.

His expression softened. "Will it make you happier than you were tonight at the Everson's ball, poppet?" As usual, her brother had attended the same event, spending his time avoiding the marriage-minded mamas. She had only seen him briefly, but he apparently had been watching her.

She blinked away the tears rushing to her eyes. "Yes. I believe so."

He downed the drink and shrugged. "Then do it." With those curt words, he offered her stunned parents a slight bow and left the room.

# 1

*October 1886*

ADELINE RAISED THE SHADE IN THE FRONT WINDOW OF HER bookstore, Once Upon a Book, making a quick note that the display needed to be changed. She generally did it the first of each month, but somehow she'd gotten busy with new inventory and had forgotten to do it.

Every month she offered the spot to one local author to showcase their books. It had helped to build her business, and the authors had been grateful for help with their sales. In turn, those authors sent their friends to Once Upon a Book.

She'd been considering forming a book club where she would invite local authors to read and discuss their books to the members. She had already started a children's reading circle that met every Saturday morning.

Addie—as she was now known in Bath—had turned into quite a good businesswoman and had never been so happy in her adult life as she'd been the past year.

After many sessions of tears and pleading, Mother had finally relented and grudgingly offered her blessing to Addie's plan. Most likely, Addie's refusal to attend any further *ton* affairs eventually swayed her. Though she doubted Mother truly understood Addie's decision. Before her father married her mother, she had been one of the *ton's* Incomparables. She had enjoyed a social life with numerous suitors, flowers, rides in the park, and dance partners. Something Addie had never experienced herself.

Father had generously bought not only the store for her, but instead of renting rooms, he'd purchased a small house at the edge of town, along with a carriage and a pair of Cleveland bays.

Addie, however, had acquired a sturdy bicycle and was proficient enough to get around town without having to make use of the carriage. She found she only used the vehicle when traveling at night since bicycle riding was dangerous after dark.

In one of the many sessions they had when considering the bookstore, Father had told her that as far as the business went, she was on her own for keeping it running. If she felt she was capable enough to take on the project, he would bow to her intelligence and capabilities and assume she could make enough money to be successful.

She was thrilled with his confidence in her, and so far, she had done quite well and was happy with the money she'd squirreled away in the bank. The one concession she'd made to her parents was to bring Mrs. Wesley with her. Mother was appalled that she intended to live alone with no chaperone. No amount of arguments on Addie's part changed her mind, so Mrs. Wesley was happily ensconced in the second bedroom in Addie's little house. Her companion and chaperone spent most of her day keeping the household running and supervising the cook and one parlor maid Addie employed.

Addie turned from the window and surveyed her kingdom. Highly polished dark wooden floors supported twelve bookcases. Half of the bookcases held non-fiction books on every subject available, shelved according to the new Dewey

Decimal system—most times. With her word blindness problem, books occasionally got mixed up.

The other half of the shelves contained novels, memoirs, poetry, and to her delight, many female authors. Miss Jane Austen, George Eliot, Mary Wollstonecraft, Elizabeth Barrett Browning, Helen Hunt Jackson, and several others held spaces on her shelves along with the popular Thomas Hardy, Charles Dickens, and Lewis Carroll.

Instead of the fussy wallpapers so prevalent everywhere, she had decided on cream-colored walls with pale green trim. The only artwork displayed on the walls were a few paintings of mostly soothing scenery done by a local artist.

Most days, the long windows along the sides of the building and the front bay window provided enough light for customers, but for evening and cloudy days, she had two pendant gas lights attached to the ceiling and a few gas lamps on small tables scattered around the room.

With feather duster in hand, Addie smiled as she dusted the shelves, lost in her thoughts, until a soft tinkle of the bell hanging over the front door sounded, alerting her to the arrival of a customer.

"Addie, where are you hiding?" Charlotte Danvers, known as Lottie to her friends, called out as her eyes swept the store.

Sticking her head around one of the bookcases, she said, "Back here, Lottie. I'm dusting the shelves."

Lottie was one of the two best friends Addie had made since her move to Bath. At the mere age of twenty, Lottie had also escaped London and its frivolity. A strikingly beautiful girl, Lottie held a secret close to her heart that she hadn't shared, even with her best friends. The only personal thing Addie and Lady Pamela knew about Lottie was that she was estranged from her mother, who lived in London.

Lottie had refused to accept any money from her mother and supported herself by giving lessons in French, social manners, polite conversation, painting, dance, and music to young ladies in Bath wishing to enter the marriage mart. All things she'd perfected while studying in France.

"Have my books come in yet?" Lottie joined Addie at the third row of books.

"Yes, it came in yesterday. I spent the entire day unloading my most recent order from London." Addie crossed her arms over her chest, the feather duster sticking up, almost reaching her nose. "How can you read those silly romance books?"

"Reading keeps me from feeling sorry for myself."

Addie studied her friend. "I know we've spoken of this before, but I think you should visit your mother."

"Subject closed." Lottie turned on her heel, and Addie followed her to the front of the store.

Addie placed the feather duster under the counter. "I have the two books you requested, so that should give you days and days of happiness." She bent over a pile of books near the front door and began sorting through them.

The bell on the door chimed once again, but Addie continued searching for Lottie's books. She continued what she was doing since most times customers preferred to walk around the store, browsing the shelves to see what interests them, rather than have the attention of the salesclerk immediately.

In the back of her mind, she fleetingly realized she didn't hear the sound of someone walking around.

"Addie," Lottie whispered.

"Yes?" She started on the second stack of books. She really should sort them better when they arrived, put categories together. But like everything else in her life, things just seemed to get jumbled up.

Lottie cleared her throat. "Addie, I think you should stop that for now."

"No. I know it's here. I remember seeing it when I unpacked the cartons yesterday." She moved to the third stack. "Just give me a minute."

"Excuse me, miss." A very deep, very male voice rumbled through the room.

Addie bolted upright, smoothing back the hair that had fallen from her topknot. "Oh, I beg your pardon, sir. I didn't see you enter."

The man frowned. "Lord."

Addie stared for a minute. "What?"

"Lord. I am *Lord* Berkshire."

Oh, good grief. Another aristocrat looking down his nose at her, most likely disapproving. She cleared her throat and assumed a more professional demeanor. "As in the Earl of?"

He nodded. Apparently speaking more than a few words at a time was too much effort for his lordship. Now that she'd gotten a good look at him, she remembered him from numerous social events years ago where he looked right through her. Berkshire represented every man she'd ever met in London.

This man, as she recalled, was a widower, and some sort of scandal had surrounded his wife's death. Since Addie was not friends with the gossipers and those 'in the know' she had nothing more than that scant bit of information. She'd always thought, however, that despite his mien of arrogance and privilege, he had sad eyes. Like an abandoned puppy.

His dark blond hair was cut in the first state of fashion. Despite the current trend for mutton chops and mustaches, Berkshire was clean-shaven, leaving his aristocratic features and the sharp lines of his jaw quite visible. His deep brown eyes regarded her with a mix of annoyance and impatience.

He was also dressed quite fashionably in a dark gray superfine wool suit, lavender and black waistcoat, and black ascot.

"Miss?" There was that slight rumble again of his voice. Deep, raspy, and . . . impatient.

She was appalled to realize she'd been staring at the man. Flustered, she said, "My apology, my lord. How may I help you?" Although she had recognized him, he apparently did not remember her at all. Which was no surprise. It was rather difficult to recall someone you'd never really looked at. But then again, one did not expect to see a lady one had met at a *ton* event working in a bookstore.

"I am in need of a book. I had hoped if you did not have what I require, you can perhaps order it for me." Goodness, the man's nose was so far up in the air, he would most likely drown in a rainstorm.

"That I can do," she said, "what book are you looking for?"

Just then, Lottie tapped Addie on the shoulder. "Excuse me. I will come back for my books later. I have two students arriving shortly."

"All right. I will have them for you when you come by for tea." She smiled and waved at her friend, then turned her attention back to Lord Berkshire, who was frowning at her.

She sighed inwardly. Patience was obviously not a strong point with his lordship. "I apologize once again, my lord, what book did you say you were interested in?"

"I am hoping to find a book that teaches sign language." His words were clipped, almost as if he disliked saying them.

Addie tilted her head and tapped her lips with her fingertip. "Sign language? I am afraid I am not familiar with that term. What is it?"

A slight slumping of his lordship's shoulders was the only indication of his distress at her words. "It is a practice over a hundred years old, but not well-known, I'm afraid. It is a way for people who are deaf to communicate with others. They use their fingers and hands to form letters and words."

"Oh, how very interesting."

He nodded, his demeanor undergoing a considerable change as he spoke. "There are even schools that teach it to children who are afflicted with deafness. It's a growing movement." His eyes were bright, and his initial stiffness gone.

She became enthralled as he continued to acquaint her

with the beginning of sign language and how it had progressed over the years. His handsome face grew even more so as he smiled—he had a dimple—waved his hands about—large, strong hands—and his body relaxed—truly a fine, admirable form.

Addie was fascinated as she watched and listened to the man. This subject was a passion for him, leaving her curious. When he stopped speaking, looking a bit uncomfortable at showing such enthusiasm, she said, "My goodness. You certainly know a lot about the subject. Is there a particular reason you find this subject so fascinating?"

He nodded, his earlier stiffness returning. "Yes. My son is deaf." He glared at her. "There is nothing wrong with his brain. He simply cannot hear, therefore, he cannot speak. He merely grunts."

She reared back at the fire in his words. This was obviously a very sensitive matter for him.

"I agree, my lord. While I cannot say I have spent time with those who are deaf, I have no reason to believe that not being able to hear results in a loss of intelligence. I am certain your boy is very bright."

His smile returned, and in truth, he looked as though he wanted to kiss her. Almost as if he read her thoughts, the very proper, high-brow earl said, "If it was not totally improper, I would kiss you for saying that, Miss..."

"Mallory. Miss Addie Mallory."

Lord Grayson Berkshire was still focused on his reaction when he first entered the bookstore to find this young lady with her nicely shaped derriere in the air as she bent over a pile of books. Since Margaret's death two years before, he had not availed himself of female company, and based on his reaction to this mere store clerk, it was time he sought some.

She was pleasingly plump, the sort of woman that always

appealed to him. Her curves were just enough to make a man comfortable embracing her. No sharp elbows poking him in the stomach or bony knees causing damage to his nether parts. This woman was all feminine cushiony softness.

Whatever sort of hairdo she had begun her day with, wisps of brown curls were already falling onto her forehead and alongside her cheeks. Her very creamy cheeks that right now were a bright red from his comment about kissing her. He had no idea where that statement had come from.

"I apologize, miss. That was not an appropriate thing to say."

She waved him off, but the glimmer in her deep blue eyes held a touch of laughter, despite her blush. A woman with a sense of humor.

"You are forgiven. However, since I am unfamiliar with sign language, you must realize I have no books on the subject. But I do receive a bulletin each month with new books that have been released. I can go through all the ones I've received since I've owned the store to see if anything presents itself."

His brows rose. "You are the owner?"

She drew herself up, but still, the top of her head only reached his jaw. "I am, indeed, my lord. I own the store." She grinned, which had him grinning back like they shared a secret of which he was unaware.

"I meant no insult, Miss Mallory, but it is quite unusual for a woman, especially at your age, to own a bookstore." He hoped he hadn't offended her because he was beginning to enjoy the young lady's company. Aside from his initial attraction to her, he found her easy to talk to and was rather enjoying their banter.

"I know what you say is true, but I have wonderful parents who allowed me to choose my own path." The smile she offered told him she did not feel wounded by his words.

"And your path is to own a bookstore?"

"Yes. I love books." Her lovely face glowed with pleasure. She was truly a happy person, someone with whom he would enjoy spending time. Considering what he was dealing with, he could use some cheering up.

"You must be a voracious reader."

Her smile faltered. "Um, not exactly." She looked sad, making him want to take her into his arms and comfort her. He gave himself a mental shake. From where were all these random thoughts coming?

Leaving him with those questionable words, she continued, now all business. "I will be happy to check my stack of bulletins. Plus, Mr. Evans, the man who sold the store to me, left a huge pile of the ones he had received over the years. I will be happy to go through them for you, as well."

Not sure why her manner changed so abruptly at his question, he was not yet prepared to finish the conversation, but it was obvious from her movements that she was ready to have him leave.

"Thank you very much. I appreciate it." He turned toward the door, and once his hand was on the doorknob, he turned back. "I would be happy to help you sort through the bulletins. I imagine you have quite a bit of work to do with running the bookstore."

Hopefully, she didn't see the desperation in him. He wanted more than anything to help Michael, especially with the threat hanging over their heads, but he would also like to spend time with this intriguing young lady who owned a bookstore.

But was not an avid reader.

She studied him for a minute, then said, "Yes, I could use the help, but I don't wish to impose upon your time."

He brightened, feeling quite silly at how happy it made him to be invited back. "I can certainly find time, and you are the one doing me the favor."

"Very well. If you wish to return when the shop closes at

six this evening, we can go over the bulletins then." Her blush told him she was most likely not used to the attention of men, which he found quite peculiar given her lovely visage and charming personality. There were many things about Miss Mallory that intrigued him, and so many questions he'd like to ask her.

"I look forward to it." He opened the door and took one step back and then looked over at her. "I won't be keeping you from some prior engagement, will I?" That was a very sneaky and subtle way to find out if Miss Mallory had a young man who would be disappointed if she were forced to work in the evening.

She gave him a slight curtsy. "Not at all, my lord. My evenings are generally free."

*Generally free.* He smiled and continued on his way.

## 2

THE NEXT AFTERNOON ADDIE STOOD BACK AND EYED THE SMALL table she'd just set with tea things. Her very favorite pink and white china teapot, along with a sugar bowl and small pitcher of milk. Three matching cups and saucers sat alongside a plate of tiny sandwiches of watercress and butter, thinly sliced cucumbers with cream cheese, and lemon tarts.

The front door of the bookstore opened, and she greeted her two friends as they entered. Every day at precisely three o'clock, they gathered in Once Upon a Book for tea. It had been their practice since Addie had been in Bath.

Lottie had arrived at the bookstore the very day it opened to introduce herself and let Addie know that as an avid reader, she would be a steady customer. She, in turn, had introduced her to Lady Pamela Manning, the third woman in their group. Another escapee from the London Season, Pamela was the oldest of the group at twenty-seven. Like Addie, she had been a veritable failure at the marriage mart and had fled to Bath right after her fifth Season, three years before.

A pretty woman, although painfully shy, Pamela also had a pronounced stutter that made itself worse when she was nervous. And she was always nervous at social events.

Unfortunately, Pamela's family did not approve of her move from London, so she made a comfortable life for herself in a lovely flat near the center of Bath, by teaching piano and voice to young ladies in order to support herself. Just as Addie was drawn to books even though reading was difficult for her, Pamela loved singing, despite her difficulty with speech. She never stuttered when she sang, and she had the voice of an angel.

The three women had cheerfully labeled themselves The Merry Misfits of Bath. They loved their lives, enjoyed each other's company, and had no need for men.

Or so they stated.

Emphatically.

Every time they gathered together.

"I have b-b-een asked to s-s-ing at a wedding!" Pamela glowed with happiness as she took her seat at the table and shook out the snowy white napkin to place on her lap. Her stutter almost never troubled her when she was with her friends. It was a sign of her excitement and probably nervousness, too, that brought the affliction back.

"Oh, how very exciting." Lottie clapped her hands. "Whose wedding?"

"Mr. Calvert and Miss S-s-shepherd from our church are getting married n-n-next Saturday. They had planned on her cousin s-s-singing, but she fell ill, and they are c-c-concerned she won't be recovered in t-t-time. So they asked me to s-s-step in."

"That's wonderful. What a great opportunity for you to show off your talent." Addie reached across the small tea table and hugged her friend.

They chatted as Addie poured tea for the ladies and passed around the plate of small sandwiches and tarts that she picked up each day from the local bakery. This was such a pleasant time for them: when Addie locked the front door and put out the 'closed for lunch' sign, while they enjoyed the food and each other's company.

"I have a f-favor to ask y-you b-both."

Lottie placed her fingers on Pamela's hand resting on the table. "Be at ease, darling. We're your friends."

"I k-know." Pamela took a deep breath. "I would l-like you both to come to the w-wedding." She looked hopefully at her friends.

Addie offered her a bright smile. "I wouldn't miss it for the world."

"Me, either," Lottie said.

"Thank you so much." Pamela let out a huge breath and took a sip of her tea. "I am very n-n-nervous about singing in p-p-public. My mother forced me to perform so many times for her friends that I swore once I moved I would never again do this. But I couldn't turn down the v-v-vicar when he asked me to fill in for the bride's c-c-cousin.

Also, there will be a wedding breakfast for the b-b-bride and groom at the church hall, where we will all be w-w-welcomed. I m-m-met with Mr. Calvert to discuss t-t-the music and asked if I c-c-could bring two friends and he s-s-said yes."

"Wonderful." Addie wiped her mouth. "I guess I will have to look through my wardrobe to find a dress appropriate for a wedding."

"Yes. Me, too," Lottie said. She swallowed the last of her sandwich and looked over at Addie. "I rode by the store last night, and you were locking up." She glanced at Pamela and smirked. "With a man."

Addie shrugged, hoping the blush she felt in her middle didn't rise all the way to her face. "A customer." She fiddled with her napkin, not meeting her friend's eyes.

Lottie looked at Pamela again, who was staring at Addie wide-eyed. "Really? It seemed the two of you were chatting away quite comfortably."

"Well, of course." Addie raised her chin, aware that her

face was most likely red as a beet. "I talk to all my customers. It's good business."

Lottie smiled and leaned back in her chair. "True. But . . . this was about a half-hour after you normally lock up."

Addie sighed. "All right. What is it you're asking me?"

Lottie leaned forward as did Pamela. "Who was the man?"

"In fact, you know him, Lottie. Well, you met him. Or rather, you saw him." When Lottie tilted her head and frowned, Addie added, "Yesterday, you were here about your two romance novels when Lord Berkshire came in."

"Oh. Yes. Now I remember." Lottie crinkled her nose. "He seemed rather rude to me."

"Not really rude. More abrupt. Or impatient, actually." She thought back to how comfortable he'd become when he began to speak about his son and his hopes to help the lad learn to communicate.

Pamela took her last sip of tea. "Since you know his name and he was here last night—past closing time—tell us more about him." She grinned. "And you."

"There is no me and him. Or him and me, rather. Or maybe it's him and I? I always get that mixed up. Anyway, he is looking for a book on sign language, and I told him I would search through all the bulletins I have from publishers on new books to see if I can find one." She looked back and forth between the two. "That's all. No mystery. Nothing like you're thinking."

"How do you know what we're thinking?" Lottie smirked, and Pam nodded.

"Because you are my best friends, and I know that look. And since there is nothing for me to tell you about his lordship, except that I am helping him find a book, why don't we change the conversation to Pamela's wedding?" She looked over at Pam. "What are you singing? Do you get to choose any of your own pieces, or are they all ones chosen by them?"

Thankfully, the ladies were willing to move onto the

wedding and what the three of them would wear. By the time they all decided on their wardrobe, it was time for Addie to re-open the store. They all hugged each other farewell. Lottie was off to the Foundling home, where she volunteered her time one day a week, and Pamela was returning home to meet her next reluctant pupil.

ADDIE CHECKED HERSELF IN THE MIRROR ONE MORE TIME AND then satisfied that she looked presentable enough for a wedding, drew on her gloves, and picked up her reticule. In light of the event she was to attend, she left her bicycle and had her carriage brought around. She would pick up Lottie and Pamela, and they would all head to the church.

Addie had been present at a number of weddings of friends, distant cousins, and even the Mallory family cook, who then presented them with her resignation the next day. The newly married woman was packed and off with her new Scottish husband to the County of Dumfries that very evening. Meals were quite dismal until Mother hired another cook.

Of course, when she was younger, Addie would sit in the church and imagine herself as the bride, and a handsome, kind, considerate-of-her-disability gentleman stood alongside her. That never happened, and somewhere over the years, she'd begun to view weddings as a reminder that it would never happen for her. But she could still be happy for the joyful couple.

This wedding, however, she was really looking forward to since her close friend would be singing. Pamela had such a lovely, sweet voice, it would be so wonderful for everyone to hear her and appreciate her talent.

The carriage drew up to Lottie's house, and her driver climbed the steps to collect Lottie. Her friend looked lovely in a pale blue satin gown with a matching wool cape and flowered hat. They chatted excitedly as they moved on to Pamela's flat.

Once again, the driver hopped down and made his way to the front door. The door opened, and they could see Pamela talking to the driver, waving her hands. After a few minutes, he nodded, the door closed, and he returned to the carriage. "Lady Pamela sends her regrets, but she is unable to attend the wedding."

The two women stared at each other, aghast. "Oh, no, she's not." Addie climbed from the carriage with Lottie right behind her as they stormed the stairs. "Pamela!"


GRAYSON ENTERED THE CHURCH WHERE HIS COUSIN, DIANA, WAS marrying a young man who he'd had not yet met, but with her common sense, he was sure her choice was just fine, and the man was not a moron. He hadn't seen members of his family in quite some time. Once the doctors had determined that Michael was deaf, and that was why the young boy only grunted instead of speaking, Grayson found himself avoiding his family, not wishing to hear their criticism or suggestions on how to deal with his son.

It seemed everyone had an opinion on what was to be done with Michael. Everything from admitting him to an asylum, to him being locked away on one of Grayson's estates with a caretaker. In other words, put the boy from his life and from his mind. Throw him away since he wasn't perfect. Nothing made him angrier than hearing those remarks.

Luckily, once he escaped from London to Bath, he found a very devoted woman to take over Michael's daily care. Mrs. Banfield read to him, pointing to the pictures in the stories, took him for walks, showed him how to manipulate blocks and form shapes with them, and insisted that he could learn just like any other child, just in a different way.

Before he began to dwell on the other threat, he pushed it

from his mind and settled into a pew. Considering how his marriage had ended, he had no great love for so-called wedded bliss, but like everyone else here, he would wish the happy couple well.

His attention was drawn to a bit of a commotion at the back of the church. He turned to see three women, two of them practically dragging the third one between them down the aisle. To his surprise, one of the draggers was Miss Mallory from the bookstore. She leaned in toward the woman in the middle and whispered something in her ear. That seemed to ease the woman, and they all made their way down the aisle.

Miss Mallory and one other woman took seats a few pews from the sanctuary. The poor woman who had been dragged down the aisle inhaled deeply and sat at the piano. She offered a tentative smile to those assembled and began to play. A few bars into the piece, she started to sing and immediately caught the attention of all those present.

Normally wedding guests would continue to talk until the bride made her appearance, but the mesmerizing effect of the woman's singing stopped all conversation. Whoever she was, she sang like an angel. He had seen her before, he was certain she had played at a few Sunday services he'd attended, but he never heard her sing before.

Within minutes, she nodded to someone at the back of the church and played the first few notes of Richard Wagner's Bridal Chorus. The congregation stood, and all turned to watch the bride make her way down the aisle. His cousin looked stunning. She'd always been a pretty girl, and she was now a beautiful woman. Of course, the joy and love on her face made her more so.

The ceremony commenced, and Grayson found his eyes drifting to the back of Miss Mallory's head the entire time.

He could see part of her profile, which he studied while the vicar droned on and on about the importance of marriage.

Things that he had believed when he and Margaret had taken their vows in this same church.

*Love, honor, and obey.*

He snorted and nodded a slight apology to the woman alongside him, who looked disapprovingly at him through her quizzing glass.

Returning his thoughts to Miss Mallory, he observed that she was one of only a few women in the church who wasn't wearing the equivalent of a bird's nest on her head. Miss Mallory's hat was a lovely sensible straw bonnet, the brim tipped up in the front with a ribbon encircling the confection and ending in a fashionable bow.

Strands of hair had escaped her coiffure, tickling the creamy skin on her neck. She sat perfectly still during the ceremony, a slight smile on her face. Was she thinking about a wedding of her own?

Soon the ceremony ended, and the guests formed a line to congratulate the bride and groom, then find their way to the church hall for the wedding breakfast. He hated to admit that he was quite pleasantly surprised when he entered the hall and found Miss Mallory and her two friends also there. Since he had spent time with her the other night going through bulletins, he felt comfortable approaching her.

After speaking with family members and brushing off their questions and suggestions about Michael, he wandered in the ladies' direction.

"Good afternoon, Miss Mallory. Ladies." He bowed slightly at the three women. Miss Mallory's cheeks turned a rather sweet shade of pink when her two companions turned to her with raised eyebrows.

"Good afternoon, my lord." She addressed her two friends. "Ladies, may I make known to you, Lord Berkshire." Both ladies offered a short curtsey.

"My lord, may I present Miss Charlotte Danvers and Lady Pamela Manning."

Grayson smiled in Lady Pamela's direction. "May I offer my congratulations on a wonderful performance at the ceremony. You truly have a lovely voice."

"T-t-thank you, my l-l-lord. I admit I w-w-was quite n-n-nervous." Lady Pamela flushed and patted her damp upper lip with her handkerchief. He ignored her stuttering, appreciating her performance even more. It amazed him that someone with that affliction could sing and never miss a note.

He shook his head. "No reason to be. You did a capital job."

"You certainly did, Pamela." Miss Mallory hugged the young woman, looking at him over her shoulder. "Thank you," she mouthed.

"Are you friends with the groom, my lord?" Lottie asked him.

"Miss Shepherd, or rather Mrs. Calvert now, is my cousin."

"There you are, Grayson. Have you been hiding on me?" Grayson groaned inwardly as his Aunt Mary made her way through the crowd, thumping her cane hard enough to put a hole in the floor.

"Good afternoon, Aunt. It is so nice to see you."

She hmphed and banged her cane again, barely missing Grayson's foot. "Not only are you hiding from me, but now you're lying to me as well. No one is ever happy to see me. One of the benefits of being old is you can make many people uncomfortable and not care because they have to keep being nice to you in case they are in your will."

She used her cane to point in the direction of the three women. "Who are these ladies?"

Of all the people who he would be forced to deal with this day, Aunt Mary was perhaps the least difficult. Although she was abrupt and what some would call gruff and snappish, she had always been his champion.

As a child, he had spent every summer with her while his parents traveled. During the other months, he was away at school. This meant he saw his parents for about a half day, once a year. Christmas morning at their enormous estate in Shire County, they would all gather in the drawing room and exchange gifts, then Mother and Father would kiss him goodbye and head to London to make the rounds of fashionable Christmas parties.

He would eat his Christmas dinner with the staff in the kitchen, who doted on him and gave him the gifts he really wanted instead of the expensive ones his parents had brought for a child they barely knew.

"May I make known to you, Miss Mallory, Miss Danvers, and Lady Pamela?" He gestured toward his aunt. "And may I present my aunt, Lady Witherspoon?"

The three ladies offered curtsies, causing his aunt to smile. Something that didn't happen all that often. "Such lovely young ladies." She poked Grayson on the arm. "You should grab one of them. It's time you put that nonsense with Margaret behind you and married again." She thumped her cane once more. "You need a mother for your boy. Someone else to see to the child's best interests, and fight on his side against your greedy relatives."

Grayson glanced sideways at the three ladies, grateful that they were talking softly among themselves, but still not sure if they were listening to Aunt Mary. "Aunt, this is not the time or place to discuss this."

"Ha! You must come for tea the next time you are in London. Send word when you will be available since I know you will complain that you are much too busy to spend time with your aged aunt." She started to move away and pointed her cane at him again. "Tea is served at precisely three o'clock. Do not be late. And bring your little boy. He reminds me of you."

The three women stopped their conversation, which led him to believe they had heard every word Aunt Mary had said since they knew it had ended. He cleared his throat. "May I escort you to one of the tables? I believe the meal is about to begin."

He extended his arm to Miss Mallory, the other two ladies following behind them. He noticed the smirks her friends cast in her direction and the slight blush again on Miss Mallory's face.

He was truly fascinated by the woman. She was obviously a lady, most likely a member of the *ton*. Why was someone like her unmarried and the owner of a bookstore in Bath?

Why did he care was the better question.

## 3

ADDIE'S FACE WOULD MOST LIKELY BE PERPETUALLY RED IF LORD Berkshire did not stop paying attention to her. The man flustered her, and she had no idea why. Well, not being stupid, there was one little thought way in the back of her mind that he might be attracted to her, but she squelched that right away as ridiculous and foolhardy.

She'd had six years to attract a suitor and failed. Miserably. Now that her life was exactly as she wanted it, a suitor would appear? Of course not. Fate would not be that unkind. That was why his attention was definitely not romantic.

He pulled out her seat, then did the same for Lottie and Pamela. As they were settling in, another couple joined them, the man no doubt related to Lord Berkshire, since their features were similar. Berkshire stood again.

"Haven't seen you in a while, Berkshire. Where have you been keeping yourself?" The man nodded briefly to Addie and her two friends. "Who are your guests?"

Perhaps because she was sitting right next to him, it appeared no one else heard the low groan coming from Lord Berkshire at the man's words. "Ladies, may I present my cousin, Mr. Samuel Newman and his wife, Emily."

She, Pamela, and Lottie all nodded in the couple's direction.

Berkshire continued. "Samuel, this is Lady Pamela, Miss Danvers, and Miss Mallory."

Mr. Newman laughed quite hardy. "And which one is yours, eh, Berkshire?" He winked. "Or all three, maybe? Wouldn't put it past you." He pulled out his wife's seat and then sat alongside her.

Addie swore she heard Lord Berkshire's back teeth grinding. "Miss Mallory and I are acquainted through her bookstore. She is searching for a book for me. Lady Pamela and Miss Danvers are her friends."

Mr. Newman leered at the four of them. "And what sort of book would that be? *Ménage à trois*? Or is there a French word for four and one? If anyone would have a term for that, it would be the French."

His lordship rose partway from his seat, his jaw tight, his fists clenched. "You forget yourself, Samuel. I demand an apology on behalf of these women." He glanced in the direction of Mrs. Newman. "And your wife, as well."

The man's face went from lascivious to disdainful. "Calm down, Berkshire. You never were one to enjoy a joke."

"To insult a woman in my presence is not a joke, and again, I demand you apologize to these ladies, or we will meet outside."

Mr. Newman attempted to keep his expression humorous, but it was obvious he knew Lord Berkshire was not making idle threats. "All right." He nodded in their direction, his smile fading. "Please accept my apologies, ladies. I meant no disrespect."

Silence fell on the group as servers began to bring out platters of food that they placed on each table. Meanwhile, footmen poured wine for the guests. Normally alcoholic beverages were not permitted in the church hall, but apparently, the bride and groom had managed to bypass that rule. They would probably have dancing as well.

After a few minutes of silence, Mr. Newman looked over at her, Lottie, and Pam and his brows rose. "Aren't you the woman who sang during the ceremony?"

Pam smiled. "Yes. It was m-m-me."

Oh dear, if Mr. Newman made a remark about Pam's stutter, Addie would be the one to jump across the table and pummel the man.

"Looks like your friends here had to persuade you to do it." He grinned, looking around the table, most likely referring to their dragging Pam down the aisle.

Lord Berkshire, Addie, Pam, and Lottie all just stared at him. Mrs. Newman kept her eyes down, appearing as though she'd never seen a plate of food before.

Realizing he wasn't going to get a response to that question, Mr. Newman shrugged and returned his attention to his meal. The remainder of the dinner was quite awkward, with only "this is delicious" to "I wonder if my cook can make this," comments floating across the table. As soon as the dessert dishes were taken away, a three-piece orchestra began playing a waltz.

His lordship folded his napkin and placed it in front of him. Turning to Addie, he said, "May I have the honor of this dance, Miss Mallory?"

A space at the front of the church hall had been set aside for the orchestra and whichever guests wished to dance. Ordinarily, Addie preferred to stay on the sidelines—where she had spent all of her Seasons and did feel a bit nervous at her dancing skills since she rarely used them.

"I am afraid my dancing skills are not up to par, my lord, Perhaps a stroll around the room?"

He pulled her chair out and took her arm. The room was large enough that they could walk the perimeter and not interfere with the dancers. After a few minutes, when they had fallen into a comfortable silence, he said, "I must apologize for my cousin. Samuel has never been one to know when to keep his mouth closed. I oftentimes pity his wife, who is a sweet woman, but you would never know that since he rarely allows her the opportunity to speak."

Before she could respond, he added, "And while I am offering apologies and penances, maybe I should include a request for forgiveness for my Aunt, Lady Witherspoon. She is my great-aunt, actually. My grandfather's sister."

That made Addie laugh. "No, please don't feel the need to apologize for her. We all have people like that in our family. I get the impression, however, that you are quite fond of her."

A warm smile graced his face. "Yes. If it weren't for Aunt Mary, I would have had no childhood at all. I spent every summer with her as a lad. She has a wonderful country estate with just enough distractions for a boy to get into trouble."

"'Ah. You were a troublesome youth, then?" Addie asked.

"Most likely no more so than any other boy growing up. For, as overbearing as she appears, Aunt allowed me to play with the servant's children." He laughed. "My father would have been appalled had he known." A flicker of sadness touched his eyes but was gone so quickly Addie wasn't sure she'd seen it at all.

In light of that pensive statement, she decided to change the subject.

"Tell me about Michael."

Lord Berkshire's face lit up immediately. It amazed her how easily his mood could change, and how visible it was on his face. The man would never be a successful card player. But his honesty warmed her.

"He is a remarkable boy. As I told you, the lad is deaf but very smart. When he reached the age of three and was still not talking, I became concerned. Not that I wasn't worried before then, but with his mother's death, I thought perhaps that was the reason for his delay."

There had been rumors when Lady Berkshire had died, but Addie had learned no more than she died under questionable circumstances. As curious as she was about his deceased wife's death, it was too much of a personal question. Despite Lord Berkshire's apparent attention to her, he still remained just one of her customers, a mere acquaintance. They hadn't even risen to the 'friends' status.

Her attention returned as he continued. "Then, I took Michael to several doctors. One in Paris specialized in children's speech problems. It was there that I learned Michael is deaf. Since he cannot hear people speaking, he could not do so himself."

He turned them in a semi-circle as they reached the corner of the room. "I blamed myself for not knowing that already." He looked down at her, his face a mask in guilt. "How could a father not know his child couldn't hear?"

Addie thought the better question was how could a mother not realize her child couldn't hear, but she kept that to herself.

"Members of my family tried to convince me that the doctor was wrong, saying Michael was an imbecile."

"I'm sorry, my lord, but I am not familiar with that word."

He hesitated for a moment. "It means deficient in intelligence. Unable to learn." He shook his head. "I refused to believe that, I still do. I have a lovely woman who lives with us, who works with Michael, Mrs. Banfield. She says he is smart and is learning at a rapid pace."

"So, is that why you decided to have him learn sign language?"

"Yes. The same doctor in Paris told me of a school there that taught deaf children, *Institution Nationale des Sourds-Muets à Paris.* It is where I learned about sign language. But I don't want to send Michael to the school in Paris alone, and I cannot stay with him since I have business here that needs my attention."

"Instead of buying a book on it, would it not be more practical to find someone who knows sign language and have them teach it to Michael? And I imagine to you, as well, if you are going to communicate with your son."

They continued to walk, their feet moving, but Berkshire continued to stare at her until she felt the very familiar flush creeping up from her middle to her face.

"That is a wonderful idea!" The tension in his body seemed to leave him, and he smiled. "If you are not careful, Miss Mallory, I will make an inappropriate statement again and suggest I should kiss you for that."

GRAYSON STUDIED THE FLUSH RISING ON MISS MALLORY'S FACE. She was such an innocent. Of course, having a man she barely knew suggest twice in their short acquaintance that he should kiss her might fluster any young lady.

He didn't understand why he was so charmed by Miss Mallory. She was pretty, of course, and had a wonderful figure, but more than that, it was her intelligence and kindness that kept drawing him in.

Much like Margaret had drawn him in before she destroyed his life. But her words had all been false. Sweet, kissable lips spewing lies. He'd sworn after his wife's death, he would never again allow a woman to worm her way into his heart, only to smash it into pieces and scatter the remnants to the wind. And laugh while she did it.

No, he would not allow that to happen again, but he could still be friends with this woman who fascinated him so. "I admire how open and accepting you are of my son's shortcomings."

She studied his face for a minute and then seemed to make a decision. "I have my own shortcomings, as well."

Just then, the music came to an end, and the couples on the floor strolled to their seats. He did not want to give up her company but didn't want to keep her from her friends if that was where she preferred to be. He might want to spend time with her, but he had no way of knowing her feelings on the matter.

He decided to take the plunge, anyway. "Would you care to continue our walk outside, Miss Mallory? I believe I could use a bit of fresh air. We could walk the path from the church hall around the rectory and then return."

It only took her a couple of seconds to smile and nod. "Yes. I believe I could use some fresh air myself."

The sun had disappeared behind clouds since they'd entered the church hall, and the air was a bit chilly. "Are you cold? We can return if you would like."

"No. I'm fine." She took his proffered arm, and they began their stroll.

A few minutes passed, and then Miss Mallory said, "I have word blindness." She didn't look at him but instead continued to stare straight ahead.

He frowned. "You have a vision problem?"

She offered him a soft smile and looked up at him. "No. It's something called word blindness. It's a strange way to describe it, but what it actually means is that I see things—words mostly—different than other people."

"I don't understand. Do you mean like color blindness?"

She blew out a deep breath. "No, not like that. I'm afraid I don't understand it very well either. All I know is when I read a book, I must go slowly because the letters switch around." She looked up at him and shrugged. "I don't know how to explain it better. What you see as the letter 'd,' for example, looks the opposite to me. But to make it more confusing, that doesn't happen all the time. Sometimes a 'd' looks like a 'd' and other times it looks like a 'b.'

"I tend to lose my place when I'm reading, so I guess the rest of the sentence. Sometimes I can only skim the page, and my eyes land on certain words which tells me what the author is saying on that page."

Berkshire let out a slow whistle and shook his head. "So that is why you said you were not a voracious reader even though you own a bookstore?"

"Yes." She sighed. "Amazingly enough, I love books. I always have. But they, unfortunately, do not love me back."

How very odd that the one person he met who showed understanding and sympathy for Michael has an issue of her own. On the other hand, there was nothing odd about it. She most likely had to deal with criticisms and misunderstanding all her life.

"Also," she continued, "I find directions confusing. What I mean is, not only left and right, but forward and backward, up and down." She offered a soft, somewhat self-deprecating laugh. "My parents were always afraid when I left the house."

What an amazing woman. Not only did she live with this unusual affliction, but she had the courage to open a business. "You are an incredible person, Miss Mallory."

She came to a halt. "Why, thank you, my lord." She flushed again and dipped a slight curtsy, apparently wanting to lighten the conversation.

"You mentioned before that your parents allowed you to live your dream to own a bookstore. Do they live in Bath, also?"

"No. They live in London. It took some persuading to convince them I would be just fine on my own. However, they insisted I bring my companion and chaperone—goodnesss, at my age, I hate that term—Mrs. Wesley."

They made their way around the rectory and headed back to the church hall. The air had grown chillier, and he was aware of Miss Mallory rubbing her hands up and down her arms.

"Would you care to wear my jacket?"

"No. Thank you very much, we are almost back to the

church hall." Almost as a second thought, she said, "I assume from our conversations you do not remember me?"

Grayson frowned. "I beg your pardon?"

Miss Mallory studied the last of the summer flowers along the path. "I have been subjected to six years of London Seasons. I have seen you with a few of your friends several times at various events."

"You have?" How could he not have remembered her?

She nodded. "Do not fret, my lord. I am not the sort of woman who gains attention from gentlemen. If you saw me at all, it was probably after I walked into a footman carrying a full tray of drinks."

He tried very hard to keep the pity from his eyes. With this woman's courage, pity was the last thing she deserved. "Ah, so that is why the escape to Bath."

"I like to think I was not escaping. I liken it to not running from but running towards."

"A very good way to think about it." They had reached the end of the path that led them back to the church hall. "Thank you for the walk. I will escort you inside, and then I will take my leave. I promised to read to Michael."

They entered the hall, the noise of dozens of conversations greeting them. The orchestra was playing another waltz, and there were several couples on the dance floor. Grayson led Miss Mallory to the table, pulled out her chair, and gave a slight bow to the others at the table. "I wish you all a good day." With those words, he turned on his heel and headed toward the bride and groom. He offered his felicitations and explained the reason for his early departure was his promise to Michael.

"Give him our love," his cousin said. Diana was perhaps his favorite cousin, one of the few who did not look at Michael as an oddity. "You must come and bring Michael for a visit once we have returned from our wedding trip."

"If I get to London, I will surely send word. Enjoy your

trip." He shook hands with Mr. Calvert, Diana's new husband, and made his way to the door.

"Be sure to make time for me, young man." Aunt Mary thumped her cane a few times as he passed her table. He bent and kissed the weathered cheek. "I will be there."

"And bring your young lady, too."

There was no point in telling Aunt Mary there was no young lady, and if he had his way, there would never again be a young lady.

*Liar.*

# 4

———

THE MONDAY AFTER THE WEDDING, ADDIE SAT AT HER SMALL desk at the back of the store, working on her ledgers. The task was laborious and with her deficiency, torturous. Once she felt the business could absorb the cost, she would hire a book-keeper. But until then, she forced herself to do a little bit of the work each day, so it didn't pile up.

Two women who had arrived together browsed the shelves, commenting to each other on various books they looked through. Another woman with a small child was going through the shelf of children's books. She really should see about ordering some more. Her children's section was gaining more and more visitors each week.

The day before, a torrential rain and windstorm had kept her from attending church, something she never did. She also had a bit of a cold and decided staying indoors with a warm toddy and a book would be fine with the Lord. Her newest read was Miss Austen's Pride and Prejudice. Even though it was an old book, she was thoroughly enjoying reading about times past.

Miss Austen had lived in Bath for a short time. Rumor had it that she didn't care for the city, but there were some spots she did enjoy. In any event, she could not have disliked it too much since two of her books, Northanger Abbey and Persuasion, were both set in Bath.

As was usual, the day after a storm brought clear, crisp air and bright sunshine. The golden rays streamed through the window next to her, bathing her in warmth and light. She looked up at the sound of the door chime. A gentleman unknown to her stepped in and glanced around.

Addie rose from her desk and walked to the front of the store. "Good morning, sir. I am Miss Mallory, owner of Once Upon a Book. Is there something particular you are interested in?"

"Yes." He grinned. "You."

She startled. "Excuse me?"

"I came to see you." He removed his bowler hat, tucking it under his arm, and gave a sharp bow. "I am Lord Featherington. My mother is a friend of your mother, and since I was making a trip to Bath for business purposes, the ladies asked if I would stop in to see you. Maybe escort you to dinner or the theater while I am here."

*Oh, Mother, no. Please, no.*

Since she never expected to see him outside of a London ballroom, she had not recognized the man immediately. Lord Featherington was known to her. Unfortunately. "How very nice of you to visit our city, my lord. How long do you plan to stay?"

He winked. Actually winked! "It depends."

She would not play into his hand and ask what his visit depended upon. "Well, I hope you have a wonderful visit. I am quite busy right now, if you would care to take a look around, I am sure we have something here that will pique your interest."

The words had no sooner left her mouth than she wanted to snatch them back. Just as she feared, he immediately used them against her. "I have already found something—or should I say someone—to pique my interest."

She groaned inwardly. Mr. Featherington was the male version of her. He was not socially adept and had a horrible habit of crashing into the things she managed to miss. She'd witnessed him falling into the Serpentine one time chasing his dog, being thrown from his curricle when he took a corner too fast, and missing the last step entering a ballroom, stumbling into Lady Montrose, bringing them both to the floor.

She could only imagine the disaster that would occur if they joined forces and stormed a restaurant or theater. She shuddered to think of the carnage.

"As much as I would enjoy dinner or the theater, I have quite a heavy schedule." She waved in the direction of the bookcases. "Running the store takes up all my time."

He shook his head and offered what she was sure he thought was a charming smile. It looked to her like a puppy waiting to be patted on the head. "I refuse to believe you don't even take time for lunch or dinner. I will pick you up here at six o'clock, which is the time your sign says you close." He waved his finger in her face. "I will not take no for an answer since I must report back to my mother upon my return to London."

*Oh, good heavens. I'll bet you do. The mothers would be waiting with bated breath.*

The only way she could refuse was to be downright rude, and her mother might very well make the trip to Bath to chastise her in person if she did. The last thing she needed was Mother visiting her again. She still had not recovered from her last visit. "Then if you insist." She gave an imitation of a smile.

"I do." He took her hand and stared into her eyes. "I will see you at six o'clock then." With those words, he turned on his heel, walked to the door, barely missing a table with books displayed on it, and left. She breathed a sigh of relief that the store was still standing.

. . .

GRAYSON STOPPED IN FRONT OF ONCE UPON A BOOK AND released Michael's hand to smooth his hair and check the rest of his appearance. Grayson could never understand how the lad could do nothing more than ride in his carriage and come out looking like he'd been rolling down hills in the park. But then again, four-year-old boys did have a way of messing themselves up. He should know since he'd been a boy once himself.

He wanted to explain to Michael that he was visiting a friend, but until he found a way to communicate with his son, he lived with the frustration of the damnable silence. He gave him a warm smile, hoping that would tell him this was somewhere pleasant.

Taking his hand once again, he opened the door to the store and entered. Miss Mallory was at the back of the store, sitting at a desk, hunched over a ledger. He walked toward her, noting four customers browsing the shelves. Grayson checked his watch again. He purposely timed his arrival near to closing time in hopes that he could persuade her to join them for dinner.

"Good evening, Miss Mallory."

She looked up, a bright smile covering her face, and bringing one to his. She must have been struggling with her books because her hair was falling down in tiny wisps near her temples and ears. There was a smudge of lead pencil on her chin, and she'd opened the top button of her shirtwaist. Yet she looked so appealing, he had a hard time finding his voice and controlling the thumping of his heart.

"I would like to introduce you to my son, Master Michael Thompson, the Viscount Falmouth."

She pushed her chair back and came around the desk to squat in front of Michael. She cupped his cheeks in her hands, laying her thumbs on his neck, and spoke directly to him.

"Such an impressive title for a little boy. Hello, Michael." Then she smiled. Of course, Michael didn't know what she said, but the smile told him all he needed to know, apparently, because he smiled back.

Grayson was stunned to see tears in her eyes when she looked up him. "He's beautiful."

Damnation, he hated how his heartbeat continued to increase, and how warm he felt inside. This woman could be dangerous to him. Yet he was drawn to her like a moth to a flame. And like a moth, if he continued to dance around her, teasing himself, getting closer and closer, he would go up in flames.

However, he did enjoy her company, and her interest in his son, so he would just need to keep her at a distance to protect his heart. And avoid incineration.

"We are ready to make our purchases," one of the customers had wandered back to Miss Mallory's desk.

"Yes. Of course." Miss Mallory laid her hand on Michael's head but spoke directly to his face. "I won't be long."

While she chatted with the customers, took money, and wrapped books, he brought Michael to the children's section of the store and pulled out a few books. They sat on the wooden bench situated along one wall near the window.

Even though he knew the boy couldn't hear, Mrs. Banfield thought they should read to him out loud. He did notice that Michael's eyes moved from the page to his mouth, back-and-forth, the entire time he read. Was he learning to lip read?

After about fifteen minutes, Miss Mallory joined them. "I think that is probably the last customer of the day."

He checked his watch. "Yes. It's almost six o'clock."

She casually fingered Michael's hair as he continued to turn the pages of a picture book. "I want you to know I have been searching, asking publishers' salesmen, and writing letters trying to find books on sign language."

He nodded. "I really appreciate that. I sent a letter to the headmaster at *Institution Nationale des Sourds-Muets à Paris.*"

"That was an excellent idea. I'm sure he can help in your search. Have you had any success in finding someone who knows sign language and can teach it to you both?"

"Since I sent that letter to Paris, I have discovered the Royal School for Deaf Children in London, which is, of course, much closer than Paris. I have sent off a letter to them, also. One thing I asked in both my letters to the schools was if they knew of someone in this area who could teach it." He shook his head and looked at his son, happily going through the pages of a book. "If I cannot find someone, I will have to take Michael to London and enroll him."

Miss Mallory handed Michael another book when he closed the one he'd been looking at. "Will you stay with him, then?"

He nodded. "I would have to. He is much too young to be left at a school with no one nearby to contact in case of an emergency. As much as I would not want to relocate to London, I would have no choice. At least I can conduct my business from there, so it would not be as much of a burden as Paris would have been." He grinned. "Except, I don't like London."

Just then, the doorbell sounded. "Oh, I hope this customer doesn't want to stay long." Miss Mallory checked her time-piece fastened to her bodice. She stood and shook out her skirts. "It is six o'clock. I will have to tell them they must return tomorrow."

"There you are. I thought you were hiding from me." A corpulent man of about thirty years strolled up to them and took Miss Mallory's hand. "I am here for our dinner date."

*Dinner date?* Grayson's stomach knotted, and everything competitive and male in him rose to the surface.

·  ·  ·

"Good evening, my lord. I didn't realize it was six o'clock already." The lie slid off her tongue like warm honey. Here she was enjoying her conversation with Lord Berkshire and his delightful little boy and totally forgotten her 'date' with Lord Featherington.

Just the thought of spending the next few hours with the man annoyed her. Not only did she have no interest in his lordship, and never would, but the idea that her mother conspired with Featherington's mother to send the man to Bath to court her raised her ire even further.

Lord Featherington looked at Berkshire. "Berkshire." He gave a curt nod.

"Featherington." He nodded back.

Of course, they would know each other since they were both peers. They eyed each other like two dogs after the same bone. In some ways, she was pleased since she'd never had that happen to her before. But she was still faced with an evening with Lord Featherington.

Suddenly, a scathingly brilliant idea occurred to her. She pulled her hand away from Featherington's sweaty one and turned to Lord Berkshire. "Would you and Michael care to join Lord Featherington and me for dinner?"

Featherington opened his mouth, she assumed to object, but good manners had him shutting it quickly. After a moment's hesitation, he said, "Yes. Why don't you and the lad join us?"

Berkshire cast a questioning glance at Addie. She gave him a slight nod, her eyes boring into him, which encouraged him to say, "Yes. That would be very nice."

"I will join you in a minute. I just need to freshen up." Addie hurried to the back room where she kept water, a comb, a toothbrush, and tooth powder. While taking care of her needs, she spent the time grumbling about Mother's interference and having to spend time with Lord Featherington.

She'd danced with him a few times at various events, and

between her mistakes and his, and his constant huffing and wiping his brow, the occasions had been torturous. At least this was just dinner, and hopefully, it would go well.

After her ministrations, she returned to the men, feeling less grubby. "I am ready."

Both men held out their elbows. She dodged them both and took Michael's hand. Featherington scowled at her. Berkshire grinned.

"Where are we dining, my lord?" Addie locked the store, then dropped the keys into her reticule.

Featherington waved to his carriage sitting in the street in front of the store. "I found a respectable little restaurant over on Wolcot Street that I thought we would enjoy." He turned to Berkshire. "I assume you have your own carriage?"

"Yes. But it probably makes more sense for us all to ride together. Don't you think?" His smirk told Addie that he didn't want her riding alone with Featherington. She still didn't understand where she stood with Lord Berkshire, or where for that matter, he stood with her. They were friends, of a sort, and now that she met his son, she wanted to help him. Other than that, she had no idea.

"If you prefer," Featherington groused. He stepped in front of Berkshire to assist her into the carriage, crushing his foot in the process. Berkshire grunted, and she wished she could explain to Berkshire that Featherington's tromping on his foot was most likely accidental.

She settled back in the seat, and once they were all comfortable, Featherington tapped on the ceiling of the carriage, and the vehicle rolled away.

Michael stared out the window while the adults remained quiet. Uncomfortable with the silence, Addie said to Featherington, "How is your mother, my lord?"

"Quite well, thank you. Your mother is still a bit distraught at your rebellion."

Addie straightened, her stomach muscles clenching. How

dare her mother refer to this as a rebellion. "This is not a rebellion, my lord. This is my life."

"Bravo," Berkshire said.

Featherington waved her off. "One I'm sure you would be more than happy to give up for marriage and a family."

Addie ground her teeth so hard they would surely be in crumbles before they arrived at the restaurant. "No, my lord. I am sorry to disagree, but I have no plans to give up my bookstore. Or my life here."

Berkshire stepped in, most likely not wanting his son to witness fisticuffs, and made a comment about the roads and the city's need to fix them. That resulted in a less threatening conversation that took up the remainder of the time until they reached Wolcot Street.

The restaurant was one Addie was familiar with but had only eaten at a couple of times. They were led to a table near the south wall, where they all settled in and perused the menu. While not exactly crowded, the restaurant had a decent number of diners.

Addie was taken by Michael, who sat quietly in his chair, watching his father's every move. When Berkshire asked Addie what looked good to her, the boy then looked over to her. Her heart broke a little bit at the confusion on the child's face. She vowed right then to help Michael in whatever way she could.

After about five minutes, the waiter appeared and took their orders. Addie just wanted the meal to be over before another contentious conversation began between her and Featherington, or one of them caused some damage to the restaurant.

"So tell me, Berkshire, how is it you survive so well here, away from London?" Featherington smirked, obviously thinking that there was no place like London to call home. More specifically: Mayfair, London.

Berkshire placed his fork alongside his plate. "I was never

fond of London. Too noisy, too crowded, too hot in the summer." He shrugged and wiped a spot on Michael's mouth with a napkin.

"What about your boy here? He would benefit from hobnobbing with the other lads of his rank." He looked at Michael, who was busy eating his food, ignoring the adults who, of course, he could not hear. "He's a very quiet one. Is there something wrong with him?"

Addie sucked in a breath at the man's audacity. She quickly looked over at Berkshire, who was calmly chewing his food. He took a sip of wine, swallowed, and looked Featherington in the eye. "My son is deaf."

"Ah. Too bad. I guess you'll have to put him away soon." Featherington continued to shovel food into his mouth, oblivious to Berkshire's mounting rage.

"I would no more put my son 'away' as you stated than Miss Mallory would sell her bookstore and move back to London." Addie could almost see the steam coming from the man's ears. It appeared if there were to be fisticuffs, it would be between him and Lord Featherington.

Featherington actually looked surprised. "I meant no insult. It's just that—"

"Perhaps we should change the conversation, my lord." Addie interrupted Featherington before he made an even greater fool of himself. "I believe the subject of England's weather or the queen's next birthday celebration are always interesting benign topics."

Thankfully, Featherington nodded, but instead of the conversation switching to something less volatile, the rest of the meal was consumed in relative silence. She finally breathed a sigh of relief when Featherington signed the bill, and they all stood to leave. She would need a tisane when she arrived home to relieve her of the pounding headache that had been served up with her dinner.

"How long do you plan to stay in Bath, Featherington?"

Lord Berkshire asked once they were all settled and the carriage on its way back to her bookstore.

Featherington looked over at Addie. "Not long." When Addie didn't look his way but continued to glare out the window at the passing stores, now all darkened for the evening, he added, "In fact, I will probably leave tomorrow."

"Good," Berkshire muttered, as the carriage rolled over the cobblestones of Bath.

5

---

"I REARRANGED A FEW OF YOUR BOOKS THAT WERE PLACED incorrectly on the shelves." Mr. Morton, one of Addie's most loyal customers, placed three books on the counter for her to wrap.

"Thank you so much. I can't imagine how they got misplaced." Addie hoped her red face didn't give away her guilt. Because of her word blindness, she oftentimes misread the book titles and authors, and the books ended up in the most peculiar places.

"I am happy to help. I am sure you have a lot to take care of, running this business by yourself." Mr. Morton was not only her most loyal customer—he claimed he never bought a book anywhere else—but he had also been one of her very first customers.

She remembered the day Once Upon a Book opened for business under her new name. Mr. Morton, with his graying hair, slight paunch, and devil-may-care attitude, had strolled through the door, looked around, smiled at her, waved his cane about, and declared, "This is my new favorite bookstore. I love the name."

He then proceeded to browse the store and purchased five

books. He also encouraged his friends to patronize the store. Yes, he was her favorite customer.

Mr. Morton picked up his books. "Well, you have a nice day, Miss Mallory." He whistled as he left the store, leaving Addie in a cheerful mood, also.

The day passed quickly, with a steady stream of customers. More misplaced books were brought to her attention. She really needed to slow down when she placed new books on the bookshelves. Most times, her mistakes were because she either wasn't paying attention to what she was doing or was rushed.

Fortunately, she had finished her ledger books the day before. She hated that part of the job because math also confused her. When things didn't balance, she oftentimes had to go back and check the numbers again. She looked forward to when she could have someone else do her books since she could very well be cheating herself.

Later that day, she was just turning her 'closed for lunch sign' back over to 'open' after waving goodbye to Lottie and Pamela when she saw Lord Berkshire crossing the street in front of the store, heading her way. His steps were brisk, his face full of determination.

Addie backed up so he wouldn't walk right into her when he entered the store. "My goodness, you seem to be in a hurry."

His hair was mussed from the wind, and she was once again taken by his handsome face with its aristocratic features, deep brown eyes with long, dark eyelashes, and full lips that were right now turned up at the ends in a slight smile.

When there were no customers in the store to keep her occupied, she foolishly spent time thinking about Berkshire in a way that was really not smart for a woman like her. She was no beauty, and her ineptness had disgraced her more than once. Did she forget how unacceptable she'd been during her Seasons? In fact, Lord Berkshire himself had looked right through her whenever she'd seen him at London events. Addie was definitely not the type of woman to whom a man like Lord Berkshire paid attention.

But since the dinner she shared with him, Michael, and Lord Featherington, she'd begun to view Berkshire in a different way. He had definitely been, if not jealous, at least a bit annoyed that Lord Featherington was taking her to dinner. It was nice to know how other girls felt when two men were vying for her attention.

Of course, Featherington had been sent by her mother, most likely with the offer of some sort of boon if he managed to pry her away from Bath, and Lord Berkshire was interested in her obtaining a book. She sighed. At least for a while, she could pretend.

Her thoughts were interrupted when his lordship came to an abrupt halt only a few feet in front of her. He reached into his jacket pocket and withdrew an envelope. "I have wonderful news!" His face glowed, which led her to believe the news was about Michael. How she would love to be the one who put that look on his face.

"What is that?" She gestured toward the envelope. "You seem very excited."

"Yes, indeed." He took a deep breath and slid the paper from the envelope and handed it to her. "I just heard from the headmaster at *Institution Nationale des Sourds-Muets à Paris.*"

She skimmed the paper as he continued, her usual way of reading something, especially when someone was watching her. "They offered to take Michael as a student, but, in the event I do not want to do that given his age, they gave me the name of an organization in London for members who communicate with sign language."

"That is good news." A sudden sinking in her stomach told her it wasn't all good news. "Um, will you be moving to London, then?"

Berkshire shook his head. "No. I do not want to live in

London. It is my hope to travel there and speak to the members of this organization to see if I can persuade one of them to move to my house here and work with Michael."

He took the letter from her hand and slid it back into the envelope. "The city is not a good place for my son. The air is much too heavy with smoke and fog. My home a few miles outside of Bath has places for him to roam, where he can climb trees and do all the other things that young boys do. He is so restricted with his deafness I would never take that away from him."

She stared at his impassioned expression, so full of excitement and love for his child. "You are a remarkable father."

To her amusement, it was his turn to blush. She let out a breath of relief that he was not moving to London, which was absolutely foolish since she had no claim on him. In fact, he would probably laugh if he knew what she was thinking. She'd been laughed at enough, thank you very much, and didn't need to mar their budding friendship by allowing him to see her foolishness. "I am very happy for you. When will you go to London?"

"It depends." He looked at her, then looked away. He seemed to be doing a great deal of thinking. He opened his mouth to speak, then shut it. Just as she was about to ask him whatever was the matter, he said, "I don't suppose you could find someone to tend to your store for a week or so?"

Very few people had the power to stun Addie into silence, but Lord Berkshire had just done that very thing. Certain she misunderstood his question, she asked, "Why do you wish to know that?"

"I know it's a great deal to ask of you, and we haven't really known each other that long, but I would love to have you travel with me and Michael to London to speak with the people in this organization. Mrs. Banfield will go, of course, as Michael's tutor, and can act as chaperone. Unless, of course, you wish to bring your own chaperone. I believe you would be quite helpful in finding the right person."

When she didn't answer because, quite frankly, her tongue was still unconscious, he added, "Mrs. Banfield is a woman in her fifties who is very conscious of proper behavior. I assume you will stay at your parents' house, not my London townhouse, of course. It will all be above board, as I would never jeopardize your reputation, I can assure you of that."

Her head was spinning with his request, while at the same time considering who she could ask to run her store for a week. The most obvious solution was to ask Pamela and Lottie to take turns. With the two of them, it would not be a huge burden for either.

"I don't know anything about sign language. Are you sure you want my opinion?" Good gracious, no one had ever solicited her opinion before, and to think Lord Berkshire wanted her to help him select a tutor for his beloved son almost brought tears to her eyes.

"Yes, I do. You are intelligent, helpful, and kind, and more importantly, Michael adores you." He grinned at the red flush that covered her face.

"He does?" Oh, if only there was a way to stop this infernal blushing. She was certainly old enough not to fall to pieces every time someone complimented her.

"Indeed." He nodded. "Even though he cannot speak, he has his own way of letting me know when he likes someone. After our dinner the other night, his excitement as he tried to let me know how much he liked you was quite amusing." He stopped for a minute, his smile fading. "And sad."

"I understand." She'd been thinking since their dinner how hard it would be to have a child you loved beyond measure and have something seriously wrong with them. An affliction that some people thought required shutting the child away.

His smile returned, a slight lifting of the right side of his mouth. "Will you go?" His eyes were warm with something she didn't want to dwell on, while his smile reminded her of Michael. Except she was certain Berkshire was much more dangerous than Michael. She was sure he used that smile to entice many a woman into his bed.

Addie tapped her lips with her finger. It would be nice to visit her parents. As a side benefit, there would be no need for them to visit her here in Bath anytime soon. As much as she loved them and was proud to show off what she'd accomplished, Mother seemed to spend her short visits to Bath trying to match her up with every gentleman who came into the store. It was downright embarrassing how she practically ambushed every man with the question, "And how is your wife today, sir?"

Lord Berkshire reached out and took her hand. "I apologize. I have probably put you on the spot, and that was not my intention."

She glanced down at their hands. His large, warm, and a bit tanned from the sun, hers small and pale. She pulled her eyes away as a slight tingle began in her middle. "No. No. Do not trouble yourself over that. I was just trying to think of how I could arrange it."

His brows rose. "Do you mean you would actually consider it?"

She looked at him, a slight smile gracing her lips. "Yes. I believe I would."

It was early morning, a week after Grayson asked Miss Mallory to accompany him to London. They were taking the train from Bath Spa Station to London. While Miss Mallory had been putting things in order at her store, he had sent a wire to the head of the organization in London, alerting him to expect their visit. He received a very encouraging response and had high hopes that he would be able to secure the services of one of its members and move them to Bath to instruct him, Michael, Miss Mallory, and Mrs. Banfield in the art of silent communication.

He had expectations of forming a similar organization in Bath. Surely there must be more people than his son who were afflicted with deafness. He refused to allow his son to grow up friendless because he couldn't talk. And if he was to put up a decent fight against the legal threat that hung over their heads, this was an important step. He did his best to shove that matter to the back of his mind since he hadn't heard any more about it for the last few weeks.

He assisted Miss Mallory and Mrs. Banfield as they alighted from his carriage at the train station. Michael jumped down with no effort, his eyes wide, his arms waving frantically as he viewed the large train. There were porters racing back and forth, assisting passengers and loading luggage onto the train that had steam coming from underneath its cars.

A woman in a very large, very colorfully decorated straw hat, holding a small white dog against her chest shouted orders to one of the porters. A man and woman embraced before the man climbed up the train stairs. The woman removed a handkerchief from her reticule, patted her eyes, then turned and walked off.

The train gave a loud blast, and porters began to speed up their movements. In all the mayhem, Michael clung to Grayson's hand, his eyes wide. This would be any small boy's delight.

His grunts in trying to tell Grayson about his excitement was drawing attention from others at the station. Some stopped and stared. Others cast looks of horror and sympathy in their direction.

From the look on Miss Mallory's face, she was just as irate as he was at the dubious attention his son was receiving. She reached out and took Michael's hand, smiling down at him. The boy calmed down, but still jumped up and down with excitement. When Grayson moved away to speak to a porter, Mrs. Banfield took Michael's hand, and the two women formed a fierce barrier between Michael and the onlookers.

Confusion continued to reign as hundreds of people swarmed the area. Grayson found a porter to assist them, and his footman and driver supervised the transfer of luggage from the carriage to the train. Panicked that he might lose Michael in the fray, he checked several times to make sure Miss Mallory and Mrs. Banfield had him safely in hand.

Michael was flushed, his eyes darting back and forth, beside himself with excitement which drew smiles from Miss Mallory. She was already communicating with him by pointing out various things, smiling, and nodding. She waved her hands around and made faces to show 'large' 'small' and 'scary.' Grayson chuckled to himself. Miss Mallory could tread the boards in Drury Lane if she wished. But she made Michael's experience much better. Asking her to join them on this journey was one of the smarter things he'd done in his life.

Shortly after they were all settled in the private car he'd arranged for, the train started up with a jerk. It continued with the unsteady movement for a few minutes until it reached a smooth ride.

A waiter arrived with the breakfast he'd ordered for them. Platters of eggs, salmon, bacon, toast, and scones were laid on a sideboard where they were to help themselves. A large pot of steaming tea was just the thing he needed.

As the train picked up momentum and left the city behind, lush green countryside passed by the window. Hills dotted with sheep grazing in the sun, small farms with vegetable gardens in the back, and flower gardens in front. A bright blue sky made it all so much more pleasing.

Having gobbled his breakfast down, Michael had his nose pressed up to the glass. Grayson noticed his grunting had now turned to gibberish, his hands waving frantically as he twisted and turned to look at Grayson and then back again to the window, pointing at things as they rode on. How frustrating it must be for the boy to see so much and be unable to share his eagerness with everyone.

After finishing her breakfast, Miss Mallory left her seat and moved next to Michael. She put her arm around his slight shoulders and pressed her own nose up against the glass. Michael turned to her, laughed, and then kissed her on the cheek. She giggled.

Grayson almost spit out the tea he was drinking. He'd mentioned twice he'd like to kiss her, but even though it was an innocent peck, his son beat him to it. Of course, were Grayson to kiss Miss Mallory, it would not be on her cheek. Nor would it be witnessed by the woman who was acting as chaperone.

No, he would take her in his arms and press her warm curvy body against his. Then he would play with her lush lips for a bit, nipping, sucking, and soothing until he covered her mouth in a kiss that would leave both of them panting with desire.

If she didn't pull back and slap his face, he would run his hands over those curves and pull her even closer until her lovely breasts were crushed up against his chest.

He sighed and returned his teacup to the table. As much as he loved the attention Miss Mallory paid his son, and loved that his son was fond of her, it was in his own best interests to keep their relationship on a friend only basis. It would be much too easy for him to view Miss Mallory, Michael, and him as a family. He was not oblivious to the pointed looks Mrs. Banfield was casting in his direction, gesturing with her head toward where Michael and Miss Mallory were conversing—in some way—about the scenery. His son's tutor had been telling him for some time that he needed a wife.

He tried very hard to convince himself that there was abso- lutely no reason why he and Miss Mallory could not have a solid friendship with no romantic involvement. He was not a young pup who couldn't control his urges, and she was a proper young lady who would never consider anything inappropriate. Therefore, he had nothing to worry about. Nothing at all.

Now, if he could only convince certain parts of his body to cooperate—he shifted in his seat—all would be well.

**6**

---

ADDIE STEPPED DOWN FROM THE TRAIN, HOLDING ONTO LORD Berkshire's hand. For as much as the pandemonium that reigned in Bath Spa Station had been difficult to deal with, the situation when they arrived in London was overwhelming. There were four times as many trains, passengers, porters, luggage, and confusion. Lord Berkshire did a fine job of keeping them all together and maneuvering them through the throngs. He had them settled in a carriage with their luggage strapped onto the boot less than an hour after the train had pulled into the station.

He explained during the train trip that he did not keep a carriage in London since he spent so little time there, and most places he visited when he was there were within walking distance, or with a short ride on his horse. Hence, he generally rented a carriage by the week while he visited.

Poor little Michael fell fast asleep leaning against Addie once the carriage moved away from the station. She put her arm around him, and he snuggled deeper into her. She smoothed her hand over his unruly curls. Slowly, he stuck his thumb in his mouth. Tears sprang to her eyes, knowing she would never hold her own child this way.

Because there would be no child for her.

She had chosen her path and was happy with it, but spending time with Michael was opening old wounds she thought she had successfully buried forever. She gave a soft sigh and looked up to see Lord Berkshire and Mrs. Banfield studying the two of them with very strange, but identical, expressions on their faces.

Of course, the ever-ready-to-spring-to-action blush rose from her middle right up her neck to her cheeks. She cleared her throat and looked out the window. It didn't matter since she could feel Berkshire's eyes still watching her. She squirmed, then concerned she might wake Michael up, she took a deep breath to calm herself and decided some inane conversation was in order.

"Have you set up an appointment yet for us to visit with the organization?"

"No." Berkshire's voice was quite raspy. Perhaps the smoke from the train or even the heavy air in London was irritating his throat. "I advised the gentleman who runs the organization that we would like to visit him, but at the time I wasn't sure when we would be able to leave Bath since we both had things needing our attention. He was quite welcoming, and suggested we contact him when we are settled, to set a definite date and time."

She nodded, but the group fell silent after that, leaving Addie again with her thoughts about children and the fact that she would never have her own.

She'd sent a wire along to her parents when she first decided to accompany Berkshire to London, so they would know to expect her. Hopefully, the fact she was traveling with his lordship would not put any ideas into their heads. She made it clear in her wire that she was accompanying him because he wanted her opinion on who to hire to teach sign language to his son. She explained that she agreed to the trip so she could visit with her parents and see some of the sights of London. She had made sure all of that was quite clear.

The hackney pulled up to Mallory House, and the door immediately opened. Mother came hurrying down the steps, her arms outstretched. Their butler came with her and opened the door to the carriage before the driver could even climb down from his perch.

"Oh, my dear, I am so very happy that you came to visit." Since she looked at Berkshire the entire time she spoke, no one was quite sure to whom she was addressing her remark. Least of all Berkshire, who glanced in Addie's direction with a slight bit of panic.

Addie slid forward on the seat. "I'm so glad *I* came for a visit, also, Mother."

She beamed at Addie and quickly returned her attention to Berkshire. "It is so nice to see you again, Lord Berkshire. Now, I insist that you all come into the house for tea."

Addie sighed. No, Mother did not understand this was a business trip with his lordship, and Addie was afraid Father was in the library with the marriage settlements drawn up, just waiting with glee for Berkshire's signature.

"We are all tired from the journey, Mother. Perhaps it would be better to let his lordship continue on to his house."

Mother sucked in a breath, which began to make Addie very nervous. The look in her eyes and the determination on her face were downright scary. Addie had seen many a marriage-minded mama during her Seasons, and at present, her mother fit the role so beautifully, Addie was ready to ask the hackney driver to return her to the station.

On the other hand, Mother more aware of social politeness than anyone she knew. In her heart, Mother knew it was best to let the others go on their way. Would good manners prevail?

"Is that our little girl?" Father joined Mother at the hackney, beaming with delight. He, also, spent more time studying

Berkshire than her. If she could crawl under the seat and never emerge, she would be the happiest woman in London.

Father stuck his hand into the carriage, reaching to shake Lord Berkshire's hand. "A pleasure to see you again, Berkshire. We hope to see more of you while our daughter visits."

"Mother, Father, may I introduce Mrs. Banfield, Master Michael's tutor." She smiled down at Michael, who continued to sleep, now propped up against Lord Berkshire. "And this is his lordship's son, Michael."

"Oh, what a darling boy." Mother shook her head. She clasped her hands against her chest and shook her head. "How much a child needs a mother."

Addie had had enough.

She was tired, travel weary, and now completely mortified with her parents' behavior. "Mother, if you will kindly step back, I would like to leave the carriage." She'd never been quite so rude to her mother, but the situation was heading toward downright ridiculous.

"Oh, of course, dear." She edged back, still studying Berkshire, who was now trying very hard to hide his grin.

After Addie left the vehicle and shook out her skirts, she turned to Lord Berkshire. "Please send round a note when you have a definite date and time for our meeting with the organization." She barely got the words out through her clenched jaw, wishing she could fall into a hole in the road and disappear, when Mother jumped right in. "Lord Berkshire, I am sure you are tired from the journey as my daughter said. But we would love for you and your son— and, of course, you as well, Mrs. Banfield—to join us for dinner this evening." Mother was not going to give up. A dog with a bone was less tenacious.

"I would enjoy that, Mrs. Mallory. However, I think it is best if Michael remains at my home with Mrs. Banfield. He is too young for the adult dining table."

"Of course. I certainly understand." She should understand since Addie was never allowed at the dining table until the year before her coming out. Mother stepped back when their butler closed the door. As the hackney began to pull away, she waved her handkerchief and quickly added, "Eight o'clock, my lord."

Addie hurried up the steps, quite sure they'd given their neighbors enough gossip to last them the next few weeks. There was no point in adding to their delight by having words with Mother on the street.

Instead of confronting her mother right away when she was so angry, Addie decided to go directly to her bedchamber. "I will be down in a little while, Mother," she said from the top of the stairs.

"That's fine, Adeline. We will have tea waiting when you're ready."

She swept into her room, the warmth from all the familiar pieces calming her a bit. The rose and cream-colored draperies and counterpane, the pale green flowered wallpaper, the soft carpet under her feet, all brought back pleasant—and not so pleasant—memories of her childhood. Not so much her years as a debutante when she returned home frustrated and feeling like a social failure. But either way, the room was comfortable and soothing.

After splashing her face with water and changing her travel half boots for a pair of soft house shoes still in her closet, she decided to beard the lion in his own den and go down to tea with her parents. If she were not to be embarrassed and harassed this entire visit, she had to let them know that Lord Berkshire was not a suitor. He was a friend. A friend in need of her help.

So what if he studied her in a way that made her insides tremble and her heart beat a wee bit faster? It mattered not that sometimes she thought his joking about kissing her was not a joke. And she did not want to consider that so many of his words and the way he sometimes studied her caused her to blush all the way to the tips of her hair.

All of that meant nothing.

She would have preferred to change out of her travel outfit, but 'twas best to get this confrontation over with, then she could strip down to her chemise and take a short nap. Stiffening her shoulders, she left her room and headed downstairs.

Her parents had their heads together, speaking softly when she entered the drawing room. Mother jumped when Addie cleared her throat. Good Lord, what were they planning now? She glanced at the paper in Mother's hand, hoping it was not the menu for the wedding breakfast.

Mother stood and gave Addie a hug. Despite her present annoyance with her mother, the familiar feel and scent of the mother who raised and loved her all her life soothed her somewhat. "It's nice to see you, Mother." She looked over at her father who rose when she entered the room. "You, as well, Father."

"You must be tired from your journey. Have a seat, and I will pour your tea."

Once the tea was fixed the way she liked it, and Mother had placed two small sandwiches and a few biscuits on a plate, Addie folded her hands in her lap and looked both of her parents in the eye. "We must speak about Lord Berkshire."

Mother sighed. "Oh, yes. His lordship. A fine figure of a man. I'm sure he would be a wonderful husband to some fortunate young lady. Father and I were just discussing him."

GRAYSON CLOSED THE BOOK HE WAS READING TO MICHAEL and kissed the sleeping boy on the forehead. He was such an energetic lad, yet he rarely stayed awake until the entire book was finished. Of course, the fact that he couldn't hear the story might have something to do with it.

Pulling the blanket up to Michael's chin, he regarded the one person in the world for whom he would give his life. Dark rumpled curls, damp from his bath, hugged his forehead. A slight sprinkling of freckles covered his nose and cheeks like fairy dust. Although he couldn't see them, Grayson knew his son's brown eyes that he'd inherited from him saw everything, lighting up with excitement over the smallest thing. No matter what it took, he would find a way to prove to the world that his son was not lacking in intelligence, only in hearing.

He knocked lightly on Mrs. Banfield's door. She opened, wrapped in a deep brown comfortable looking robe. "Are you leaving now, my lord?"

He nodded. "Yes. Michael is asleep."

"Have an enjoyable evening then, my lord." She closed the door softly, and Grayson made his way down the stairs to the entrance hall where Brooks, his butler at the London townhouse, stood with Grayson's coat and hat.

After donning his outdoor attire, Grayson left the house and strode to the mews, at the back of the row of townhouses, to retrieve the horse he kept in London. After mounting Reggie and tossing a coin to the lad who tacked the horse for him, Grayson made his way to the street and headed toward the Mallory townhouse in Mayfair.

The evening should prove to be quite interesting. It was obvious that Mr. and Mrs. Mallory were brimming with delight over the fact that their daughter arrived in London with an earl in tow. He shook his head and chuckled at poor Miss Mallory's reaction to her parents' obvious attempts to make a match right there on the spot. He would have to be careful this evening, or he might be served a marriage contract right along with dessert.

It would be foolish to pretend he had no interest in Miss Mallory beyond her help with Michael. Or that he hadn't thought about her in a carnal way. She was delightful company and possessed a body a man would thoroughly enjoy. One he could spend hours caressing and discovering all the places to make her hum.

She'd already shown genuine interest in Michael, and the boy had studied her with adoring eyes throughout the entire trip from Bath. There was no doubt in his mind that she wouldn't make a delightful bed partner and mother to his son. There was just one problem.

For as much as he liked and desired her, he did not love her and did not want to love her. Ever. That sort of entanglement had destroyed him once before. Never again. However, he doubted with Miss Mallory's loving and caring nature, she would accept a husband without love. It would not be fair to offer marriage to her when it would eventually make her miserable.

His thoughts kept him busy until he realized the short ride from his home on Arlington Street to Mayfair and the Mallory townhouse had ended. As he drew up to the front of the house, a man ran from around the back and took his horse. "I'll take good care of 'im, my lord."

Grayson tossed a coin at the man. "Feed and water him, if you will." The man tugged on the brim of his cap and led the horse away.

The townhouse was in a row of houses, very typical of the area. It appeared to be one of the larger ones, with at least twelve rooms. The marble steps leading to the front door were worn in the center from all the feet hurrying up and down over the years.

Grayson straightened his ascot and made his way to the front door, which was immediately opened by a pleasant looking butler before he'd had the chance to drop the interesting knocker. "Good evening, Lord Berkshire." He bowed. "You are expected."

Grayson shrugged out of his coat, handed his hat to the butler, and followed the man down a well-lit corridor. The townhouse had been tastefully decorated, the wallpaper lining the entrance and corridor a pale rose and green. The highly polished wooden floor was covered with a plush sage green runner that muted their steps. Gas lights had been installed on the walls to replace the normal candle sconces. In all, his impression of the Mallorys was of a family with good taste, one that did not display avarice. They stopped at a dark oak pocket door that the butler slid open.

"Lord Berkshire," he announced.

Mrs. Mallory hopped from her seat as if kicked from behind. Mr. Mallory stood, and his daughter joined him. "Good evening, my lord. We are so very happy you have joined us for dinner," Mrs. Mallory simpered, a bright smile on her face and most likely wedding bells ringing in her ears.

"Berkshire." Mr. Mallory crossed the room, holding out his hand, which Berkshire shook. "Brandy?"

"Yes. That would be fine."

As the man poured drinks for them all, brandy for the men and sherry for the women, Grayson remembered what he knew of the family. Mallory was the third son of the Earl of Lindsay. With two older brothers, there was never a strong chance that he would inherit, and since his oldest brother had already produced three sons, it was a moot point.

Mrs. Mallory had been a baronet's daughter and had been declared an Incomparable the year she made her come-out. Due to her beauty and charm, she'd married the son of an earl. While not perfect, since he had no title, it had moved her up a bit on the social ladder.

In addition to Miss Mallory, there was a son, Marcus, who Berkshire knew from Eton, although Mallory was four years behind him in school. They also belonged to a few of the same clubs; however, Grayson spent very little time at his London clubs since his marriage ended and he'd relocated to Bath to lick his wounds.

"Adeline tells me your son has a hearing problem." Mrs. Mallory took a sip of her sherry, but appeared to be genuinely interested, not just making conversation, which relaxed him a bit. He was always a tad on the defensive side when the subject of his son was brought up.

"He is deaf." Might as well call it what it is. "The doctors don't believe he can hear anything at all. They are not certain if he was born that way, or if it occurred due to a childhood illness."

"I understand it is your purpose in making this trip to visit with an organization of deaf-mutes here in London," Mr. Mallory said, leaning forward, his brandy glass dangling between his spread legs.

"Yes, sir. I have been in contact with the man who heads up the group, and he has agreed to meet with me—and your daughter—to provide us with information and names of those who might be interested in teaching my son sign language."

Mrs. Mallory studied her drink, running her fingertip over the rim. "How interesting that you requested Adeline to go with you." She took a sip and smiled at him, saying no more.

Ah. Now was the time to be very careful. Mrs. Mallory had a look upon her face that had been directed at him numerous times from numerous mamas in numerous ballrooms before he married Margaret, then again after he'd come out of mourning. "I respect her opinion, and she has shown a great deal of interest in my son—"

"Oh, yes," Mrs. Mallory jumped in, "Adeline just loves children. Don't you, dear?" She patted Miss Mallory's hand then looked back over at Grayson. "She would make a wonderful mother. And wife, of course." She smiled in his direction; her eyes bright with . . . something.

Miss Mallory made a slight groan, and he downed the rest of his brandy in one gulp.

## 7

ADDIE SUFFERED THROUGH THE DINNER WITH HER PARENTS AND Lord Berkshire, barely choking down her food as Mother raved on about her accomplishments—very few—her social graces—absolutely none—her love of children—what woman doesn't love children?—her household management skills—Mother never let her do any of that—and, what a wonderful wife she would be. Groan.

To his credit, his lordship swallowed every bit of nonsense she threw at him, right along with the roast beef and potatoes. He smiled and nodded so much he began to look like a marionette with Mother pulling the strings.

"Adeline, why don't you show his lordship our gardens?"

"It's raining out, Mother."

Her mother glanced out the window at the downpour, the rain pelting against the window like pebbles. The wind whipped the trees, the last of the autumn leaves scattering over the yard. A flash of lightning lit up the room. "Oh, yes. I had not noticed." She turned to Lord Berkshire. "Adeline just loves flowers."

"And thunderstorms," Addie mumbled.

Lord Berkshire choked on his tea.

"In that case, I insist you entertain us with the pianoforte, Adeline." She beamed at his lordship again. "Adeline sings like an angel."

*No, Mother. I sing like a pig frantically racing from the butcher's knife.*

"My throat is a bit sore, Mother. Perhaps we can just retire to the drawing room. Maybe play a game of cards or chess?"

To her eternal gratefulness, Berkshire wiped his mouth and placed his napkin alongside his plate. "I am afraid I must return home, Mrs. Mallory. I have things I must do this evening to prepare for my meeting with my man of business in the morning."

Mother's shoulders slumped slightly, and her brilliant smile lost some of its glow. "Oh, how very sad. Not that your meeting is sad, of course," she quickly added, "but we would have enjoyed your company much longer."

"Maybe he can move in," Addie spoke so softly that only Berkshire could hear her. He grinned.

"I must thank you for the charming company and wonderful dinner. Your cook is to be commended." He pushed his chair out and stood.

"We are having a dinner party next week. You must attend. Just a small gathering."

"Dinner party?" Adeline asked.

Mother glared at her. "Yes, dear. Remember? I told you about it earlier." Her smile would give nightmares to a young child.

*Can one die of embarrassment?*

"My lord, did you bring your carriage?" Mother glanced out the window, finally acknowledging the ferocious storm raging beyond their walls.

"No. Actually, I rode my horse."

"I insist you take our carriage. We can arrange to have your horse delivered back to you tomorrow."

Berkshire offered a slight bow. "Thank you. I appreciate that kindness."

Now it was Mother's turn to blush. In her unnerved state, she turned to Adeline. "See his lordship out, dearest." She poked her in the arm. No doubt Addie would be black and blue in the morning. Rubbing her arm, she stood as Berkshire drew her chair out.

They left the dining room and headed to the entrance hall. "I am so, so sorry for my mother."

"No need," Berkshire said, as he accepted his hat and coat from Grimsley. "My mother was not much different. I think there is something about the birthing process that turns normal, lovely women into scheming matchmakers extraordinaire. Some of the mothers I have encountered would have made excellent field marshals during the Napoleonic wars. We might have defeated him sooner if they had."

They chatted for a few minutes until Grimsley announced the carriage awaited him in front of the townhouse. Berkshire turned to her once he had shrugged into his coat. "May I call for you tomorrow to take a ride with me and Michael? I'm hoping the weather will clear by then, and he might enjoy Hyde Park." He took the umbrella that Grimsley held out to him.

Now, why did her heart take an extra thump? Was it the way he looked at her? The closeness of his body? The familiar light scent of bay rum and starched linen that always drifted from him? "Yes, I would like that." Her voice came out breathy. For heaven's sake. Apparently, Mother was not the only woman in the family who could embarrass herself.

Berkshire glanced out the small window next to the front door. "If the rain continues, perhaps we can take him to one of the museums."

She nodded, suddenly unable to form words as she looked into his dark brown eyes, similar to the lovely chocolate she drank each morning. She'd never noticed the golden specks before.

"Would two o'clock be acceptable?"

"Yes." She cleared her throat since the word came out a squeak.

He studied her for a minute as if thinking about something and started to reach out to her. Then he glanced at Grimsley standing there, staring straight ahead, pretending not to notice them. Berkshire nodded briefly, turned, and left the house.

Addie closed her eyes and pinched the bridge of her nose. The headache forming at the back of her head was slowly making its way up to encompass her entire head. What she wanted more than anything was to climb the stairs, order a hot bath and a tisane, then sleep. But Mother had to be dealt with, or this visit would turn into a disaster.

"Mother, I think you frightened Lord Berkshire." She entered the dining room just as her parents were rising from the table.

"Nonsense." They both sat back down, most likely ready to do battle. Mother shook her head. "If you want to bring the man up to scratch, you have to move forward. It never hurts to do a bit of nudging."

"Nudging? Mother, you practically slammed him over the head with a hundred-page marriage contract. And there is no 'bringing him up to scratch.' I explained to you before that I am only here with his lordship to provide an opinion on who he might hire to teach his son sign language."

Mother pointed her finger at Addie. "Do not fool yourself, young lady. I saw the way he looked at you. And he certainly needs a mother for that poor little boy. And it would solve your problem, as well."

"What problem would that be, Mother?" Addie held her breath, fearing what her mother would say, but knowing in her heart what she would hear.

"You, working at that store. You could give all of that up and take your proper place in society. I'm sure Lord Berkshire would love to once again live in London and assume his parliamentary duties."

"No. In fact, Lord Berkshire prefers to live away from London. As far as his parliamentary duties go, he is apparently able to attend to them from Bath." Addie took a seat and poured another cup of tepid tea, rather than ask for a fresh pot to be brought. Maybe it would help her headache.

Her mother drew her always present white-laced handkerchief from the sleeve of her dress. She patted the corner of her dry eye. "I don't understand you, Adeline. Every woman wants the financial security of marriage and a home of her own."

"I have security, and I have a home."

"I want to see you settled before I die."

Drama. "Mother, I am settled, and I am certain you have many more years to live." *And badger me.*

"But you don't understand." More patting of her dry eyes. "I want grandchildren before I am too old and feeble to lift them."

Addie wondered for a minute how rude it would be to bang one's head on the dining room table. Too rude, for sure.

"Mother, you know I love you. And Father, as well. However, right now, I am very tired from our journey today and would like to retire. I beg you not to be quite so 'enthusiastic' with Lord Berkshire. He is in London for a specific purpose. To find help for his son. That is why I am here, as well, to help him help his son."

Mother patted her hand. More dry eye patting with her other hand. "Very well. I imagine you are fatigued. I will have Molly—our new maid—draw a bath for you and send up a tisane."

Addie let out a deep breath. "Thank you." She stood and kissed her parents on the cheek. "I wish you a good night, then."

Just as she reached the door to the corridor, Mother said, "I made an appointment for us to visit the modiste in the morning to have a new gown made up for you for our dinner party next week. I am sure Lord Berkshire would think you quite lovely in a pale rose gown."

Addie held in the scream that wanted to rip from her throat.

GRAYSON CHECKED HIS TIMEPIECE, THEN TUCKED IT AWAY IN THE small pocket on his gray and black striped vest. Two o'clock. Right on time.

He hurried up the steps to the Mallory townhouse, grateful for the bright sun that had followed the storm the night before. The sunshine matched his spirits, and he found himself whistling as he walked, his spirits high. He tried not to believe it was because he was going to see Miss Mallory, but a little bit of honestly refused to allow him that deception.

Yes. He did like Miss Mallory. A lot. But it could never go further than that. The fact that Michael took an instant liking to her only helped. Or made it worse, depending on how one looked at it. He did not want to fall in love again. Once was enough when it ended the way his marriage had.

Michael and Mrs. Banfield waited in the rented carriage for him to collect Miss Mallory for their ride to Hyde Park. The grounds would be too wet to stroll, but they could take a nice ride and then maybe stop for tea at Gunter's.

The butler had the door opened before his foot reached the top step. "Good afternoon, my lord. Miss Mallory is expecting you. Please follow me to the drawing room."

Grayson tried very hard to remain a gentleman and not groan when he saw Mrs. Mallory waiting for him, perched on the arm of the sofa. She popped up and broke into a huge smile when the butler announced him.

"Good afternoon, Mrs. Mallory. Are you having a pleasant day?"

She held her arms out to him as if they were long-lost relatives. "Yes, quite pleasant. Especially now that you have arrived."

Not sure if she intended for him to take her hands, or if she was—shudder—going to hug him, he stepped back and elected to take her hands. "You are looking well."

"Thank you, my lord." She turned to a small table alongside the sofa and picked up a cream-colored envelope and held it out to him. "Here is your invitation to dinner next week. It will be a small gathering."

Grayson sighed inwardly. He'd forgotten how members of the *ton* thought a *small* gathering was the size of the House of Lords. "Thank you. I look forward to it."

*Liar.* He'd rather bang his head against the wall for a half hour than attend a dinner party with members of the *ton*. He'd never enjoyed life in London, preferring instead a quiet life in Bath or at his country estate. Margaret had always wanted to attend as many events as she could during the Season, and then again during the holidays.

His ideal evening was sitting in a comfortable chair next to his fireplace, a glass of fine brandy in his hand, Michael sitting at his feet playing with his toys and . . .

He would not allow himself to add the final component. Yet, his brain did not cooperate, and it shouted: *Miss Mallory sitting across from me, reading a book, or working on her sewing.*

It was then that he realized Mrs. Mallory had been speaking to him. Luckily his automatic responses, learned from childhood, was to nod and smile.

"So you agree?" Mrs. Mallory broke into a brilliant smile.

Blast. What had he just agreed to?

"I am sure you will enjoy this new actor. From what I've read, he is quite good in *The Two Gentlemen of Verona*."

Dear God. *Two Gentlemen of Verona*, what he considered to

be one of the worst of Shakespeare's plays, and from what he'd heard, he was not alone in his assessment.

"I am sure I will." Luckily at that moment, Miss Mallory arrived to rescue him from her mother before he promised any number of things for which he had no time.

"Good afternoon, my lord." Miss Mallory was a vision in loveliness as she swept into the room. Her mother's eyes lit up as she studied her daughter.

"You look lovely, Adeline." Mrs. Mallory directed her beaming bright smile in his direction. "Doesn't she look wonderful, my lord? That carriage gown is stunning."

"Yes. Indeed." Despite her mother's annoying match-making attempts, Grayson was sure he had just given the woman even more ammunition by how he also regarded Miss Mallory. Except he wasn't admiring how winsome she looked in her carriage gown, he was imagining how she looked underneath all the layers of clothes she wore.

The vibrant lavender of her gown hugged her waist and hips, emphasizing her lovely curved figure, and turned her deep blue eyes violet. A sweet little matching hat sat on top of her head, black netting falling over her forehead. A few ringlets had been left to dangle alongside her cheeks, with the rest of her hair drawn back in a chignon.

When Mrs. Mallory cleared her throat, he realized he'd been staring at her daughter with a hunger like a green youth.

"Where's Michael?" Miss Mallory pulled on black kid leather gloves and smiled up at him.

*Michael?*

For the love of God, he had to pull himself together before he made a complete arse of himself. "He is waiting in the carriage with Mrs. Banfield." He turned to Mrs. Mallory, who regarded him with a very dangerous looking smirk. "That is Michael's tutor. She will act as chaperone."

"Oh, I don't think there is a need for a chaperone at Adeline's age." She waved her hand in dismissal, leaving him with the belief that she hoped Adeline would be compromised to hurry up the wedding he had no doubt she'd been planning since his arrival.

"Oh, if he's been waiting all this time, we should hurry." Miss Mallory took the few steps to her mother and kissed her on the cheek.

As they reached the front door, Mrs. Mallory hurried after them. "Please take tea with us when you return, my lord."

Miss Mallory came to an abrupt halt, and he swore he heard her teeth grinding. "Actually, Mother, we are stopping at Gunter's for tea, so that won't be necessary." She then gave his back a very unladylike shove toward the open door. "I will see you later."

Once on the steps, Grayson reached into the open door and took Miss Mallory's cloak from the butler, who seemed confused by how quickly she was out the door. Once the door closed, he placed the cloak over her shoulders.

The air outside seemed clearer. Lighter. Easier to pull into his lungs. How the devil was he going to spend time with Miss Mallory without feeling as though every time he stepped over her front doorstep he was walking into the lion's den? If this visit lasted much longer, he expected to be greeted by a vicar the next time he called. He was certain Satan on a prowl for souls was not as tenacious as Mrs. Mallory.

"Look what I have." Miss Mallory held up a small cloth bag.

"What is that?" He took her elbow and assisted her down the steps.

"Bread pieces. I thought Michael would enjoy feeding the ducks."

"That's a wonderful idea," Grayson said. As they reached the bottom step, Miss Mallory turned and looked up at him, genuine concern on her pretty face. "My lord, I'm afraid I must once again apologize for my mother, and I would certainly understand if you wish to meet with the organization and other matters without me." She reached for his hand as he helped her into the vehicle.

"No. I want you to accompany me. That was the plan." He climbed in after her, noting that Michael was already climbing on her lap, a huge grin on his face. "Please don't worry yourself over your mother. I assure you I can handle mothers."

Miss Mallory adjusted Michael on her lap, offering him a kiss on his cheek. "Good afternoon, Mrs. Banfield."

"Good afternoon." Mrs. Banfield looked at Grayson with raised brows. He grinned back. Apparently, she was just as impressed as he was with how Michael had immediately abandoned her to go to Miss Mallory, and she had then made him comfortable on her lap as if she'd done it numerous times before. If anything was going to move him in the direction Mrs. Mallory was so frantically pulling him toward, it would be Michael's obvious adoration of her daughter.

"I found a book in my father's library about deafness." Miss Mallory ran her hand up and down Michael's arm. "One of the things mentioned was how touch is so very important to anyone suffering from deafness."

Another point in her favor. Not that he was looking for points. He still thought a marriage between them would not be in his best interests. He could easily fall in love with Miss Mallory, and he'd only just put his heart back together. He doubted it could survive another blow.

"May I borrow the book?"

She now wove her fingers through Michael's curls, and all he could imagine was her doing the same to him. How it would feel to have her delicate fingers touching him. In more places than just his hair.

"Yes. Of course."

He had to stop and remember his question. Oh, yes. The book. "Thank you."

Mrs. Banfield asked Miss Mallory about her gown, and the rest of the trip was taken up with the two women discussing fashion while Grayson watched, mesmerized, as Miss Mallory and Michael formed an attachment that was both good and bad news.

Once they arrived at Hyde Park, they rode until they reached the Serpentine with the coach coming to a rolling stop. Grayson stepped out, turning to help Mrs. Banfield and Miss Mallory. Michael was so eager he was jumping up and down. It reminded him that the boy needed more stimulation since he couldn't hear. Once they returned to Bath, hopefully with a promise from a tutor to work with Michael, he would have to be sure his son had more outings.

With Miss Mallory. Because Michael cared for her so much, he told himself.

Miss Mallory took his son by the hand and led him toward the lake. She pulled out some bread from the bag and showed it to him. Then she broke it into little pieces and threw them to the ducks that had climbed from the water, waddling toward them. Then ducks came from all directions, causing Michael to clap his hands and shout.

She handed him a few pieces, and he tossed those. It was a peaceful few minutes until Miss Mallory turned to say something to Grayson, and Michael immediately dashed to the water, splashing as he reached for one of the ducks.

Grayson and Miss Mallory shouted, "Michael, stop!"

Then they turned toward each other. "He can't hear us." They raced to the water just as Michael's head disappeared.

# 8

---

ADDIE REACHED THE WATER AFTER LORD BERKSHIRE, WHO HAD scooped his son up from the lake sputtering and howling. Michael's arms waved frantically, and he pointed over to the water, grunting.

"It is quite chilly, my lord. We must leave immediately and return Michael to your home before he develops an ague." Addie hurried alongside the man as he huddled a wailing Michael to his chest. Seeing them coming, the driver had the carriage door opened before they even reached the vehicle.

Addie climbed in first and took Michael from Berkshire's arms. Mrs. Banfield had a heck of a time catching up to them and arrived at the carriage out of breath. Once she was in, with Berkshire behind her, his lordship slammed the carriage door, and the driver took off.

Addie clasped Michael to her chest as Berkshire fumbled out of his wool coat and handed it to Addie, who wrapped it snugly around Michael. The little boy's body was cold and saturated. She rubbed her hand over his arms and legs trying to warm him up.

He had stopped crying and lay in her arms, sniffling and shivering. Addie looked over at Lord Berkshire, who was still and pale as snow. Mrs. Banfield shook her head as she regarded the boy. "We should not have gone to the park. 'Tis best if we keep him safe at home."

"No!" Lord Berkshire's outburst had both Addie and Mrs. Banfield staring at him. "I do not want to continue to treat my son like a freak. Aside from his lack of hearing, he is a normal little boy with all the eagerness and curiosity of any child. I won't deny him a childhood because he might hurt himself. Even with a perfect sense of hearing, any child could have fallen into the water."

Mrs. Banfield sniffed her disapproval, but Addie applauded his decision. It proved again to her that Berkshire was a loving man who genuinely cared for his son.

That led her to wonder about the previous Lady Berkshire. Addie knew very little about her, except that Berkshire did not like to talk about her.

Although the trip to Berkshire townhouse was not more than a few miles, it seemed to take forever with Michael shivering in her arms. The cold water from his clothes seeped into her clothing, bringing on her own shivers. The two of them together were practically rocking the coach.

Once the carriage arrived, Berkshire didn't wait for the driver to open the door, but jumped out and took Michael from Addie. The two women followed him up the stairs and into the house. An older and quite staid appearing butler opened the door.

"Brooks, have a hot bath drawn as quickly as possible." Berkshire took the steps two at a time with Addie and Mrs. Banfield right behind him. As focused as she was on Michael, Addie did take time to notice the somewhat garish decor of the entrance hall and the stairway. The deep red flower-striped wallpaper almost gave her a headache. Gold colored carpet led them to a bathing room at the end of a corridor.

"Mrs. Banfield, can you please ask one of the maids to find something for Miss Mallory to wear?" Berkshire set Michael on his feet and began to rip the boy's wet clothing off. "She will need to change into dry clothing."

"That is not necessary, my lord. I can have the driver see me home." Addie barely got the words past her chattering teeth. Her chin was numb with cold, and her hands were freezing.

Berkshire shook his head and lifted Michael into the partially filled tub. "No. That will not do at all. By the time you made it home, you would be completely chilled."

"My lord, there are still a few of Lady Berkshire's gowns here. I imagine one of them will fit Miss Mallory." A young maid entered the bathing room.

"Miss Mallory, go along with Sybil, she will find something for you to wear."

Before Addie had a chance to thank him and insist upon being on her way, the young but quite strong maid took her by the arm and led her away. Mrs. Banfield left, presumably to return to her room, and Berkshire was busy sloshing warm water over his son.

Addie was not generally the superstitious type, but wearing a dead woman's clothing did make her a tad uncomfortable. She was pleasantly surprised when the dress the maid gave her fit. Until Sybil mentioned the gown was one her ladyship wore during her confinement. Thankfully, it was quite loose around Addie's waist but fit her perfectly around the bust.

It was a lovely gown, more tasteful than the house's decor. The deep blue silk flattered her complexion. Beautiful black embroidery had been stitched along the bodice, sleeves, and hem. As she dried herself with the towel that had been warmed by the fire and dressed in Lady Berkshire's gown, Addie thought about Michael's mother.

She knew from *ton* gossip that some sort of scandal surrounded her death, but nothing more than that. Addie wasn't even sure if she had ever met his lordship's late wife.

Was she beautiful? Did she possess all the grace and charm that Addie did not, which allowed her to marry an earl?

Sybil returned to the bedchamber that Addie had used to dress and led her to the drawing room with instructions from Berkshire. Sybil explained that she should take tea, and he would join her as soon as Master Michael was settled in a nightshirt with a glass of warm milk and biscuits.

Tea arrived only a few minutes before Berkshire. "How is Michael?"

Berkshire took the seat across from her, with a tea tray filled with small cucumber, watercress, and smoked salmon sandwiches, and an array of biscuits and tarts between them.

Berkshire accepted the cup of tea Addie handed him. "Michael is in much better shape than I am." He shook his head and popped a small sandwich into his mouth.

"These things are generally more difficult for the parent than the child. I'm glad he is better, though. I would not want something like that to put him off other adventures."

"That will not happen. I've allowed Mrs. Banfield to make a great deal of the decisions with regard to Michael since I was at a loss as to what to do for the lad." He shook his head. "I will no longer permit that. I am the boy's father, and I say he needs to be exposed to more of the world."

"If you are able to secure the services of a tutor for him, he will be presented with a whole new way of looking at his world." Addie took the final sip of her tea.

GRAYSON STUDIED MISS MALLORY AS SHE WIPED HER MOUTH with a napkin and placed it alongside her plate.

"Is that one of my late wife's gowns?" Margaret had never looked so good in that frock, although, if he remembered correctly, she wore that during her confinement.

"Yes," Miss Mallory said. "I was surprised it fit me, but

then Sybil informed me that the deceased Lady Berkshire made use of this particular gown before she gave birth."

"I must say it looks far better on you."

Miss Mallory sighed. "I take it Lady Berkshire was slender?"

Grayson nodded and leaned back in his chair, continuing to study her. "Margaret had the form of a stick. The only time she looked really well in her clothing was when she was increasing with Michael. You, on the other hand, have enough—"

"Pounds?"

"Nay. Enough curves to fill out gowns properly."

He smiled at her raised eyebrows. "Thank you, my lord, now if you will excuse me, I think it is time for me to go home. If you could have your carriage readied, I would appreciate it."

He tossed his napkin down and stood, circling the table and smiling when her eyes grew wide at his movement. He reached out and took both her hands in his and pulled her up. "I have a feeling that you find yourself lacking in masculine appeal."

She just stared at him, her eyes wide, her mouth agape. Then she slowly nodded.

"You are wrong, Miss Mallory. I am very much a man, and I find you to be of a fine form. You are possessed of curves that would drive a man wild. Myself included."

"I don't understand . . ."

"Understand this. I've wanted to do this since I first laid eyes on you that morning in your bookstore." Before he could change his mind, he cupped her cheeks in his hands and lowered his mouth.

Miss Mallory sucked in a sharp breath as his mouth covered hers. She held herself stiff until he slid his tongue along her sealed lips, and she opened. His invasion was swift and complete. He pulled her closer, all her soft warmth and luscious curves pressed up against him.

She was everything he had expected. Soft, warm, willing, and eager to learn. She gingerly touched the tip of her tongue to his, and the heat exploded throughout his body. Unable to hold his hands still, he ran his palms over her back, cupped her round buttocks, and pulled her against his hardness.

Miss Mallory—Addie, as he would think of her from now on—was an innocent, but she was no meek young girl. She allowed her own hands to roam over his back and shoulders, then allowed her fingers to play with the hair at his nape.

Grayson pulled back and scattered kisses over her jaw, neck, and the soft, sensitive skin under her ear. "You are so beautiful, so responsive." Wandering into territory he should not traverse, he moved his hand to cup her generous breast. He rubbed his thumb over her already erect nipple. There was a soft moan. He wasn't sure if it was him or her.

Addie sucked in a breath. "Oh, goodness, my lord. That feels wonderful."

His tongue circled her ear, then he tugged gently on her earlobe with his teeth. "Grayson. My name is Grayson." He blew softly into her ear. "Say it."

"Grayson." The word came out soft, whispery.

"My lord, Michael requests you read him a story." Mrs. Banfield's voice cut into his passion charged brain. "Oh, dear."

Addie shoved him away and stared at him aghast. "My lord!" Her face was bright red, and she was having a hard time accessing air, making her lovely breasts rise and fall.

Having had more experience with getting caught at inconvenient times, Grayson looked over at Mrs. Banfield, who was grinning.

"Thank you, Mrs. Banfield, Please tell the lad I will be up shortly."

She nodded and left the room. He looked at Addie, her palms covering her face. "Oh, I am humiliated. And ruined."

Grayson gripped her elbow. She pulled back. He tried very hard to suppress his laughter because he knew she was embarrassed. But he felt elated. Wonderful. Excited. It all felt so right. She felt right. What he was going to do about it remained to be seen, but now he had to calm her down or she would march out of his life forever.

"Addie, please don't be upset. I'm sorry that Mrs. Banfield interrupted us—"

Addie moaned.

"—but I am not sorry I kissed you. As I said, it was something I wanted to do from the moment we met."

Addie looked up at him and took a deep breath. "Can you have your carriage brought around? I think I should go home."

"Very well. But I will not send you home, I will escort you." He was not about to let her go after what happened so she could dwell on it and probably sell her bookstore and move back with her parents.

She shook her head. "No. Michael is waiting for you."

"While the carriage is made ready, I shall visit with him and explain, as best I can, that I will read him two stories when I return." Before she could object again, he took her by the elbow and walked her to the front hall. "Grimsley, please have the carriage brought around. I will be escorting Miss Mallory home."

Grayson bounded up the stairs, happier and more energetic than he'd been in years.

THE FOLLOWING DAY GRAYSON MADE HIS PROMISED VISIT TO Aunt Mary. Although she had requested—nay ordered—him to bring Addie when he attended the she-dragon for tea, he arrived on Aunt's doorstep at precisely three o'clock by himself on the day he had sent word to expect him.

"Is that my neglectful grand-nephew?" He only needed to follow Aunt Mary's voice to know she awaited him in the drawing room.

"It is I, Aunt. I have arrived just on time as you requested," He strolled into her domain, once again wincing at the decor. The wall coverings, carpets, fussy paintings, and dozens of trinkets were so much Aunt Mary that she needn't even been sitting there for him to feel her presence,

He bent to kiss her wizened cheek, the familiar scent of apples and cinnamon drifting from her. Just the smell brought back pleasant memories from his childhood.

"If memory serves, and it generally does, despite my age, I requested you to bring your son and your young lady." Aunt looked around him as if she expected them to jump out from behind.

He wasn't exactly sure why he hadn't brought Addie, except the kiss they shared the other day had left him feeling wonderful, but at the same time oddly out of sorts. He wasn't quite ready to give a name to his feelings and was afraid Aunt Mary would do so before he was ready.

Ready for what he didn't know.

"Michael took a slight dunk in the Serpentine yesterday, and I am keeping him in bed for a day or so to make sure he doesn't develop an ague. Miss Mallory was unable to join us." He took a seat across from her just as the door opened and a footman entered pushing a tea cart.

"Pish! How is it your young boy ended up in the Serpentine? Isn't that guardian you employ watching him carefully enough?

"It was an accident, and Miss Mallory and I were there with him, as well."

"Ha! I am willing to bet *Miss Mallory* was unable to come because you never invited her. I should never have left it up to you. The next time I will send an invitation." While she chastised him, Aunt directed the footman to place the tea servings on the small table between her and Grayson. "There are a few things I wanted to ask her."

"That's what I was afraid of," he murmured.

Aunt pounded the floor with her cane. "Speak up, lad. Age has not affected my memory, but it seems to have played a game with my hearing." She leaned in. "Unless what you said was not intended for my ears, eh?" She cackled like the witch in one of the storybooks she had read to him as a child.

Once she poured the tea and passed around the biscuits and small sandwiches, she said, "I am happy to see you moving on, you know."

Grayson almost choked on his tea. "Who said anything about moving on?"

Aunt Mary studied him over her cup of tea, and her wrinkled face softened. "It's time, young man. Margaret is dead, and her treachery died with her."

"I don't wish to talk about it." Although he was quite sure that was precisely what his aunt had in mind when she invited him.

He'd spent many a long night going over in his head how he could have missed the fact that his wife was having an affair with his brother.

His own brother!

After the first few months of their marriage, Grayson had recognized that Margaret was restless, didn't seem to settle into a normal married routine. But he loved her, and so he never saw—or didn't want to see—her discontent.

When she became pregnant with Michael, he thought that would all end. The thought of her body swelling with his child, and then holding the babe to her breast filled him with awe and happiness.

But motherhood had been no more appealing than marriage.

After months of complaining about her fatigue, nausea, and her growing stomach, she had a very easy birth and had gladly handed over the care of their son to a wet nurse and nanny. She pestered him relentlessly until he agreed to leave Michael at his estate in the country and travel to London for the Season. His brother Peter and his wife, Beatrice, soon followed them.

For months he tried to pretend that everything was fine, that Margaret was just a high-spirited woman who needed the dressing up, gossiping, balls, parties, and everything else that he had been only too happy to give up for a peaceful married life.

And he loved her.

Except he'd been blinded by that love. And betrayed by his brother.

He still remembered the numbness that filled him when he read the note she'd left for him. She was leaving the country with his brother, Peter. He barely had time to digest that information when a member of the London Metropolitan Police arrived at his front door with the news that the carriage they were running away in, had crashed into a brick wall on a sharp turn.

Killing both of them.

"Stop brooding, young man." Aunt Mary pulled him out of his meandering. "Your wife was a harlot and your brother a cad. Put them behind you and think about your son."

Grayson ran his fingers through his hair. "Ah, yes. Michael."

"A sweet boy who I rarely see." She scowled at him and took another sip of tea.

Grayson grinned. "You would frighten him into nightmares."

She dismissed him with a wave of her hand. "What is happening with Peter's widow and her foolish claim against the boy?"

He knew Aunt Mary would bring that up as well. "Nothing right now. My solicitor says she has no chance of succeeding in having Michael declared incompetent and having her son, David, step up as my heir presumptive."

"Another reason to marry again, Grayson. If you produce

another son, her claim would make no difference. Even if she succeeded in having Michael declared incompetent, another son would nullify her claim."

*Marry again.*

What, at one time, had been an idea easily dismissed, now did not seem so horrible. Perhaps Addie had something to do with that. Truth be told, she had quite a bit to do with this change in thought.

He could see himself married to her. They could have a pleasant relationship with respect and fondness.

Addressing his aunt's statement, he said, "I feel sorry for Beatrice. She was as much a victim of Peter and Margaret's treachery as was I."

"Bah!" She thumped her cane with relish. "You are too kind. Being betrayed by her husband has no connection to trying to strip a little boy of his future by declaring him incompetent. If anyone is incompetent, it's that dimwitted son of hers."

Grayson's nephew, David Hartley, was a spoiled, incorrigible lad who, at only ten years had already been sent down from Harrow for disciplinary reasons, after he practically killed another student in a fight.

"Go get yourself married, Grayson. Get your wife with child and produce another son. That will end her nonsense and make you a happier man."

When he remained silent, she added, "And your son a happier lad."

## 9

THE DAY OF THEIR MEETING WITH A MEMBER OF THE organization who they hoped would help Michael had arrived.

Addie didn't understand why she was so nervous, but her palms were damp, and she kept patting her upper lip with her handkerchief as Grayson's carriage made its way through the streets of London to the home of Mr. Gerard Simmons who lived outside of Mayfair.

Grayson appeared as tense as she felt. He kept adjusting his ascot and clearing his throat. Mrs. Banfield and Michael appeared oblivious to the entire matter, with both of them sitting and staring out the window. Michael crawled over Mrs. Banfield and cuddled on Addie's lap.

In such a short time, she had already grown to love the little boy. He had Grayson's eyes, hair, and strong jaw. He would be a handsome man one day. The intelligence and curiosity in his eyes told her he had a very good chance of making a successful life for himself, despite his deafness.

They pulled up to a lovely townhouse, which had a white door with black trim. A metal snake's head sat in the middle of the door with a knocker attached. Grayson helped her and

Mrs. Banfield out of the coach and took Addie's elbow. Mrs. Banfield held Michael's hand.

They started up the steps but didn't get far when the front door opened. A stately looking man, wearing the household livery, opened the door. He was probably somewhere in his fifties, and from the looks of his form, he didn't miss many meals.

His face was pleasant, and he smiled as they entered. "Good afternoon. Mr. Simmons awaits you all in the drawing room. If you will follow me." He proceeded to lead them down the corridor past two closed doors. At the third door, he paused and gave a slight knock before sliding the pocket door opened.

"Sir, your guests have arrived."

Mr. Simmons rose from the chair he occupied behind a very large desk where several books were spread open. He was a pleasant man, much younger than Addie would have guessed.

His dark blond hair was mussed as if he'd run his fingers through it many times. He had deep brown eyes, and a slight scar on his upper lip. His frame was sturdy but slender. When he smiled, slight wrinkles appeared at the corners of his eyes and alongside his mouth, which told Addie he smiled a great deal.

His demeanor immediately relaxed her.

He rounded the desk and approached them. "I assume you are Miss Mallory?" He took her extended hand, gave it a slight squeeze, then turned to Mrs. Banfield. "Mrs. Banfield?"

She blushed and nodded. Next, he shook Grayson's hand and then turned his attention to Michael. He squatted in front of him and looked him in the eye. "Hello."

Michael looked from Mr. Simmons up to Grayson. When his father nodded, the boy looked back at Mr. Simmons and smiled. The man took Michael by the hand and led him to a small glass case that held several butterflies. He pointed to one of the butterflies and turned to Michael. He then crossed his two hands across his chest, with the palms facing his body. He linked his thumbs and made a waving motion with his hands.

Michael studied him intently. Then Mr. Simmons pointed to the butterflies again and then gestured to Michael. The little boy looked confused, but Mr. Simmons did the same thing again. He helped Michael place his hands in the proper position and showed him how to wave his hands.

He had him do it three more times. Then he took him by the hand and walked him to the desk where he took one of the books off the pile. He closed the book and pointed at it. Then he held his hands together, palm-to-palm, and holding his pinkies together, he opened his hands as if opening a book.

Michael watched him do it a few times. Then Mr. Simmons pointed to Michael and then gestured to the book.

Without hesitation, he imitated what Mr. Simmons had done, then looked over at Grayson with a bright smile on his face.

He understood!

The lesson continued with Mr. Simmons showing Michael different things in the room and then using his hands to indicate the object. Addie was amazed at how quickly Michael understood what they were doing.

She, Mrs. Banfield, and Grayson all shook their heads in amazement at all the things Michael was able to name using his hands. After about fifteen minutes, going back over what they'd done, Mr. Simmons patted Michael on the head and handed him a small piece of candy.

He indicated the chairs in a grouping in front of the fireplace. The adults had all been so entertained, they had stood the entire time watching Mr. Simmons and Michael.

Once they were settled in and Michael happily engaged with his sweet, Mr. Simmons said, "My lord, your son is extremely bright. Did you say he was aged four years?"

"Yes. Last May."

Mr. Simmons smiled softly. "And I am quite sure there were those who attempted to have you believe he was an idiot."

Grayson scowled. "Yes. That is correct." Then he turned to gaze upon his son with all the love and pride a parent felt for their child who had just successfully mastered a new and difficult challenge. "But I always knew they were wrong,"

Addie looked over at Mrs. Banfield, who was patting the corners of her eyes. Addie felt a lump growing in her own throat, as well.

Mr. Simmons returned to his desk and drew a note pad from the middle drawer. Dipping his pen into the inkwell, he asked, "When was your son's hearing last tested?"

"About a year ago, when he was still not speaking, I grew concerned. My physician conducted some sort of a test and determined he was deaf."

"In both ears?"

Grayson fidgeted in his seat. "I assume so. You must excuse me, Mr. Simmons. I made the mistake of believing at first, as everyone else was trying to tell me that the lad lacked intelligence. Then I was so relieved when I learned it was deafness that kept him from speaking, I accepted it and did nothing further."

Mr. Simmons nodded and continued to write. "Do you remember what sort of test the doctor performed?"

"It was quite simple, really. He just turned Michael away from him and made various noises."

Mr. Simmons shook his head and tsked, but kept busy scribbling in his notepad. "Several years ago, Mr. David Edward Hughs began using an audiometer. With your permission, I would like to set up a meeting with my doctor who has the machine so we can test your son and see if we can determine the degree of deafness he suffers from."

"That would be wonderful," Grayson said, glancing over at

Addie, who grinned at him. This meeting was going so well that all her nervousness had faded.

They talked some more, and then when they were ready to depart, Mr. Simmons took Michael by the hand and walked him to the center of the room. He gently grasped the boy by the chin so he was looking directly at him. He then made the sign for butterfly.

At first, Michael just stared at him, then he smiled and raced over to the glass case and pointed to the butterflies. Mr. Simmons continued on until Michael had identified all the items he'd taught him.

"Yes, my lord." Mr. Simmons said, patting Michael on the head. "A very bright boy. I will be in touch with the name of a few individuals willing to take on the job of teaching your son."

Two days after the meeting with Mr. Simmons, Addie awaited Grayson, who was escorting her to a ball. Once it had become known that Lord Berkshire had returned to London, the invitations had begun to pour in with frightening speed. He begged her to attend with him.

The regular Season had ended, but those left in town preparing for the holiday season kept up a social whirl, albeit a smaller one. Even though Grayson's wife had died two years before, he had not attended any *ton* affairs.

Although he hadn't said as much, a young, handsome, wealthy, and titled man was a dream come true to marriage-minded mamas and their daughters who had not brought a gentleman up to scratch during the regular Season.

Why Grayson imagined she would be a deterrent to these ladies remained a mystery to Addie. She'd never held the attention of a man during her Seasons and to think any woman would believe he was courting the London failure was ludicrous.

But it would be nice for a change to appear on the arm of a sought-after lord as if such a thing happened to her all the time.

Addie checked herself in the mirror and adjusted the bodice of her gown. The dark wine-colored velvet frock was fitted at her waist and snug around her breasts. The edging of the square-cut bodice and cuffs of the long sleeves had been decorated with gold embroidery,

How Mother had managed to get a gown made within a few days was surely a miracle. Addie could just imagine what her mother had paid for it in either coin or promises.

Agnes, her mother's lady's maid, had done up Addie's generally untamed hair into a respectable upsweep hairdo that she braided pearls throughout. Mother had lent her a beautiful ruby necklace and matching earbobs.

She'd never looked so good, even though she hadn't shed a pound. With how tight Agnes has pulled her stays, the gown looked wonderful, but Addie was already finding it hard to breathe. As little as one country dance and she would collapse from lack of air.

"Miss, your gentleman has arrived." Agnes blushed and giggled as she made her announcement from Addie's open bedroom door.

Before Addie could mumble, "He's not my gentleman." Agnes was gone. Addie sighed and picked up her gloves and reticule. She gasped as she bent over. This was going to be a difficult night.

Of course, Grayson was closeted with Father in the library when Addie arrived downstairs. Most likely suffering an inquisition as to his income, investments, properties, and overall general health. She would not be surprised to see Father examining Grayson's teeth.

She swept into the room to see Father and Grayson sitting comfortably in two chairs facing the fireplace, sipping on brandy as if they'd done it for years.

Both men stood as she entered. Grayson's eyes swept over her, his smile growing as he regarded her, then bowed. "You are looking lovely this evening, Miss Mallory."

"Thank you, my lord," Addie made a slight dip, which was as much as she could handle without passing out.

Mother hurried into the room. "Oh, good. You haven't left yet." She sailed across the room to stand in front of Addie. She lowered her voice. "This could be your opportunity. Men love to walk in dark gardens with ladies."

Addie sputtered. "Mother, whatever do you mean?" Surely, she wasn't telling her to get herself compromised. Really. Sometimes Mother went just too far.

Mrs. Banfield had been acting as her chaperone for the trip, but since she was still responsible for Michael, she did not attend evening events. But then, with Addie being an acknowledged spinster and a businesswoman, there wasn't much that could damage her reputation.

"Just making a suggestion, dear. No need to get yourself at sixes and sevens."

"Would you care for a sherry, Adeline?" Father held up the sherry decanter.

"We have time if you wish," Grayson said.

And give her mother more time to say inappropriate things.

"No, thank you."

Grayson downed the rest of his drink and placed the empty glass on the table next to him. "Then we shall be off."

Once they reached the front door, Grayson took her cloak from Grimsley and placed it on her shoulders. The night air was chilly, and the area shrouded in fog. They made their way down the stairs to Grayson's carriage.

"Have a lovely time, dear," Mother called from the door.

GRAYSON HAD ALMOST SWALLOWED HIS TONGUE WHEN ADDIE

entered the library earlier. The gown she wore hugged every single curve on her luscious body. The deep red brought out the creaminess of her skin. But more than that was the surprise he saw on her face when he complimented her.

She'd mentioned that she had very little success during her Seasons, which baffled him. There should have been hordes of men pursuing her. Why she hadn't been plucked from the group of young ladies was baffling.

They settled into his carriage and began the short trek to Lord and Lady Stevenson's townhouse for the ball. After adjusting her skirts, Addie cleared her throat and looked him in the eye.

"My lord—"

"Grayson."

"Yes, of course. I believe I explained to you that I am not the most graceful person at a ball."

"Yes. You did mention something about walking into a footman."

She looked so desolate that he wanted to pull her into his arms, settle her on his lap and tell her whatever problem concerned her, he would fix.

"I mix up things in my mind. When the dancers are to move in one direction, I can be counted on to go the opposite. It has made more than one partner frustrated, as well as the other dancers in our circle."

"I see." He tried not to smile, but her earnest expression reminded him of a small child trying to explain herself out of trouble. "Go on."

"That is all. Actually, 'tis one of the reasons I left London almost a year ago and settled in Bath. I was not very successful."

Grayson shook his head. "I do not agree with you, Addie. You moved from your family home to live in another town and opened a bookstore that you run very well. How do you figure you are not successful?"

"You are missing the point. I am unsuccessful in a ballroom. I am a social tragedy."

He could hold it in no longer, he laughed, only to immediately regret it at the slight blush on Addie's face, and the stiffening of her shoulders. "'Tis not funny."

He gave in to his compulsion and reached across the space separating them and pulled her to his side. Not on his lap as he would have preferred since he felt that was a bit improper.

"If dance steps confuse you, then we shall not dance anything but a waltz."

"That would be scandalous if we danced a waltz more than once."

"Then we shall dance only one waltz and spend the rest of the time socializing."

Addie shook her head, the misery on her face continuing. "No. You will be required to dance with the other young ladies because it's expected. Plus, you are a prime candidate for the marriage-minded mamas."

He blanched at the thought of all the young ladies and their mothers who will be making a final attempt at an engagement before the next Season began. "Then I shall do my duty and dance with a young lady or two. But . . ." he took her chin in his fingers, tilting her head "you will dance a country dance or two with me. I will keep you going in the right direction."

Before she could answer, the carriage drew to a rolling stop in front of the Stevenson home. There was a short queue, and they had barely gathered their things—Addie quickly moving to the other side of the carriage—before the door was opened by a footman. "Good evening."

He extended his hand, but before Addie could reach for it, Grayson jumped out, forcing the footman to move aside. Then he reached out for Addie's hand.

She accepted, and he placed her hand on his arm, and

they made their way up to the Stevenson home. Grayson noticed the tightening of Addie's hand on his arm.

He was quite annoyed at the dimwitted gentleman of the *ton* when Addie told him about her failure on the marriage mart. Despite her lack of grace, how could such a pretty woman, with charm and wit, not have dozens of offers for her hand? The men in London were dolts to be sure. On the other hand, them passing Addie by left him in a position to consider her for a wife. Yes. He had finally realized that having a wife and mother to champion Michael was the best thing he could do. Aunt Mary was correct, it had just taken him a little while to admit it. And if he were to consider taking the one step, he swore he would never take again, Miss Adeline Mallory was the one.

Of course, he had no idea how she would take to his proposal, but he hoped she would see the rightness of it. Despite her independence, she needed a man. All women did. She could even sell the bookstore and spend her time managing his estates and helping with Michael.

As a smart woman, she would be more than open to having a marriage of two like-minded people who would develop a warm, friendly relationship with no messy entanglements such as love. Perhaps he had underestimated her when he thought a loveless marriage would make her miserable. She was far too intelligent, he assured himself.

After handing their coats to the footman at the door, he and Addie arrived at the reception line. "Lord Berkshire! I cannot tell you how very happy we are that you accepted our invitation." Lady Stevenson practically fell over, trying to reach across her husband to grasp Grayson's hand.

"My lady, it is indeed a pleasure to see you again." Grayson turned to Addie. "I assume you are acquainted with Miss Mallory?"

Lady Stevenson's face fell. "Oh, yes, indeed. How are you, Miss Mallory? I thought I heard you had moved to Bath?"

Before she could answer, Lady Stevenson turned back to Grayson. "My lord, my charming niece Lady Diana is visiting with us." She moved out of the reception line and took him by the arm. "I just know she would love to meet you."

He opened his mouth to speak but was quickly whisked away while Lady Stevenson recited all her niece's qualities. He turned as he entered the ballroom to see Addie staring after him.

## 10

————

ADDIE WATCHED LADY STEVENSON DRAG GRAYSON AWAY BEFORE Lord Stevenson had even addressed her. The soft smile he offered her helped a bit. "It appears we are just about finished with the receiving line, Miss Mallory. May I escort you into the ballroom?"

What was she to do? She'd been through this so many times before. Left on her own at social events. But she was not the same Miss Mallory who skulked away like a frightened bird or hid in corners behind ugly plants. She was a business owner. She lived on her own. She made important decisions every day.

She raised her chin and accepted Lord Stevenson's arm. "Thank you, my lord."

She could have sworn he mumbled, "well done" as he took her hand and placed it on his arm. Addie glided into the room, ordering herself to stop shaking. Taking a deep breath would help, but given her stays, that was unlikely. At this point, she would consider the evening a success if she didn't faint.

Lady Stevenson had dragged Grayson over to a lovely woman, the one who must have been her niece.

Addie's new-found confidence slipped a bit when she

regarded Lady Diana. She was tall, willowy, and dressed in a gown much too low cut for an unmarried lady. She clung to Grayson's arm and gazed up at him as if he knew the secrets of the universe and was about to share them with her. She resembled every woman who had disdained and dismissed her over the years.

It looked as though Lady Diana was not going to have Grayson to herself, though. Two other ladies drifted over in their direction. While Addie spoke with Lord Stevenson and two of his cohorts about the price of grain feed, and the problem of losing tenants to the factories, Grayson was soon surrounded by ladies. Not that she noticed, of course.

Some of them were 'leftovers' from the other Seasons, a few she remembered from her torturous time in London. Naturally, the ever-present bored matrons and widows looking for a man to warm their bed flocked to his side as well.

Even though she had been escorted to this ball by a very handsome gentleman, she was right where she'd been all the years of her Seasons. Off in a corner. The only difference was she was speaking with gentlemen old enough to be her grandfather, instead of women old enough to be her grandmother.

Hopefully, she could avoid stumbling into something or dropping a drink on herself—with help—which would make this evening a mild success. The last thing she wanted to do was embarrass Grayson.

The orchestra started up a waltz, and all the ladies hanging onto Grayson stared up at him with adoring eyes. So many lashes fluttered, it was amazing his hair stayed in place.

Addie shook her head at the nonsense, then her eyes grew wide when he murmured something to the ladies surrounding him and broke away from the group. He walked squarely in her direction, causing her to turn to see who he was headed toward. Nothing behind her except the large, very ugly plant she wasn't hiding behind.

He crossed the room, his demeanor very much like a

young, powerful lion stalking its mate. Her heart began to pound, and for some peculiar reason, she felt the need to flee. Then she reminded herself this was Grayson. He was harmless.

Wasn't he?

"I believe this is my dance, Miss Mallory?" He bowed before her and took her hand. She felt the heat from his hand right through his glove and hers. "Close your mouth, my dear, or I will be forced to kiss you. 'Tis very tempting, don't you know?"

He grinned when she snapped her mouth shut.

"Why . . . why are you dancing with *me*?" Addie looked around him at the gaggle of women glaring at her. It was hard for her not to smirk. She was with one of the most handsome man in the room. She was the one who took him away from the beautiful, popular, and much-sought-after women.

"I told you we would waltz." He took her in his arms and moved her onto the dance floor. "I don't see why you are surprised."

He was as graceful and accomplished waltzing as he was in everything else. The women who had been glaring at her were now putting their heads together, glancing in her direction with amazement.

The wallflower had won.

"But there were so many beautiful and graceful women hanging on your arm."

He raised his brows. "And?"

"Well, I just thought . . . Oops, sorry." She had stepped on his foot when she turned the wrong direction.

"Addie. Look me in the eyes. Do not look at your feet." He pulled her a bit tighter. "Yes. Like that. Don't worry about what your feet are doing, just relax and let me guide you,"

Amazingly enough, it did make it easier for her to follow while staring at him. But it also made her insides tingle, especially the tips of her breasts and the area between her legs.

He increased the pressure on her back to tell her how to move. She sighed. If only Grayson had been her dance master, she might have been a bit more successful on the dance floor.

However, continuing to look in his eyes was not a good idea. The burning she saw there both frightened and excited her. Her face grew flushed, and the heat from his body radiated out to warm her like a raging fireplace.

He pulled her even closer as they turned. She felt graceful, charming, and happy. She was dancing! And not tripping all over her own feet or her partner's. She laughed with absolute joy.

"I love seeing you laugh. You don't do it enough, you know." Grayson's lips moved in a crooked smile that made him look like a little boy. Except this was no little boy holding her in his arms.

She really needed to get control of herself. She was growing warmer by the minute, and her stays were pinching her something dreadful. If only she could take a deep breath, she might stop the lightheadedness that this dance was bringing on.

Oh, heavens. Supposed she fainted right here in Grayson's arms on the dance floor for everyone to witness? She glanced up at him.

"Addie, are you unwell?" He studied her with concern.

"Why do"—she panted—"you"—she panted again—"think I am"—more panting—"unwell?"

He continued to stare at her, his eyes narrowing. "Maybe because you are growing paler by the moment, and you seem to be having a hard time breathing."

Damn. He noticed.

"Addie?"

Luckily, he slowed them down. She leaned in. "I cannot . . . breathe."

Rather than ask any more questions, he swung them around and right out the patio door, which blessedly was open since the room had grown quite warm despite the cold air outside. He moved them off into a corner. "Why can't you breathe? Are you ill?"

There was no way she could get out of this. It was either tell him of her dilemma or collapse at his feet, which would raise all sorts of alarms. Despite the embarrassment, she whispered, "My stays."

He leaned in. She couldn't be sure because it was dark, but she had the awful feeling he was grinning. "Your stays?"

Rather than use up the bit of air she was able to drag into her lungs, she merely nodded.

"Come." He wrapped his arm around her shoulders and half walked, half carried her several yards along the patio to another door that he opened and walked her through. It was a dark room, and from what she could see among the shadows, it must have been Lord Stevenson's library.

The lightheadedness was growing as her vision dimmed. Before she succumbed to the encroaching swoon, he whipped her around. "Too tight?"

She nodded, misery and embarrassment flooding her until she thought perhaps fainting might not be such a bad thing.

Grayson quickly undid the back of her gown and loosened the strings to her stays in a flash. Trying not to dwell on how adept he was at the task. Addie took in the first real breath of air since she'd gotten dressed.

She covered her face with her hands and wished the ground to open up and swallow her. "I am so sorry." Even she could hear the tears in her voice. She wouldn't blame Grayson if he left her here in the library and returned to the charming women whose company he'd left to dance with the wallflower.

"There is nothing to be sorry for." He took her wrists and removed her hands from her face. "Addie, why in heaven's name did you allow yourself to be abused in such a way?"

She still refused to look up at him but stared at his ascot. "It was the only way I could fit into the gown."

*That is what happens when you are plump, and your mother refuses to acknowledge it, and orders a gown made in the size she wishes you were.*

Grayson placed his knuckle under her chin and lifted her head. She was forced to look into his eyes. She didn't see the expected pity or distaste, but amusement. "Sweetheart, don't ever do that again. You are lovely just the way you are." He ran his hands down her sides and then, with his hands wrapped around her waist, pulled her close until their bodies were touching.

The tingling she felt on the dance floor returned. It was the same warm, exciting, frightening feeling as before. She licked her lips as Grayson lowered his head and gently covered her mouth with his.

A kiss that started out soft and tender soon turned into so much more. Grayson plundered her mouth, moving one arm up around her shoulders and the other at her waist, pulling her flush against his hard body,

His warm, muscular, hard body.

Someone moaned, and she wasn't sure if it was her or him. He ran his tongue along the seam of her mouth, nudging her to open. His tongue swept in, and he shifted so he could cup her cheeks, tilting her head in such a way that he took the kiss even deeper.

The sound of voices coming from the corridor outside the library door was like a bucket of cold water. They pulled apart, but the top of her gown, which was still loosened, slipped off her shoulders. Addie grabbed the bodice and held it up.

"What will we do? We can't stay here much longer. Surely we will be missed." There was no doubt in her mind that all the ladies surrounding Grayson were waiting with a great deal of impatience for his return. With growing panic, Addie continued to clutch the bodice of her gown, but it kept slipping down. They could be in serious trouble if caught. This did not look good.

.   .   .

GRAYSON ASSESSED THE SITUATION. HERE THEY WERE IN A DARK library with Addie's gown undone and her stays unlaced. Well, he had already decided that marriage might not be such a bad thing, and Addie was certainly his choice. If discovered, everything pointed to a quick betrothal and wedding.

"Yes, we are in a pickle. I have no idea how many guests saw us leave the room. We have to return to the patio and go back into the ballroom that way."

Addie pulled back. "What!" She looked at him panic-stricken. "We cannot walk through the ballroom like this. I am only half-dressed."

"I shall give you my jacket," He shrugged out of the garment and placed it over her shoulders. "And simply say you grew chilled while on the patio."

"And I am to spend the rest of the evening like this? Eventually, I would no longer need your jacket. It's quite warm in that room." She shook her head. "No, I must return home."

She looked toward the heavens as if invoking a greater power to help them. "This is a disaster, which is normally how my attempts at social events turn out. There must be a way for me to leave without being seen at all. That shouldn't be hard since I am quite unnoticeable anyway."

Grayson smiled softly. "I will not argue that point right now, but despite your thoughts about your anonymity, we were seen on the dance floor together. Who knows how many people watched us leave through the patio doors? If we don't return soon, I am afraid the amount and type of gossip that follows will not be pleasant."

Addie gave a quick nod of her head, her lips tightened with determination. "We shall leave through the garden. If anyone questions either of us after tonight, we merely say I took ill, and you escorted me home."

Grayson pinched the bridge of his nose. "Addie, the only

way out of the garden is to climb over the fence." He raised his brows. "Are you prepared to do that?" Meanwhile, his mind was in a whirl trying to think of a way out of this, but every idea led him right back to a quick betrothal and wedding.

What amused him more than anything was his almost delight at that result.

"I would happily *crawl* over the fence than walk through that room with my gown undone and wearing your jacket." Addie's voice cracked, and she had begun to shiver. He drew her into his arms, his heart twisting at her distress, but she was correct, things would not go well if they entered the ball-room together with Addie in such disarray.

The couple who had passed by the library door had moved on, and the strains of a country dance floated from the ballroom. Addie looked up at him. "There is only one way. You must re-fasten my gown."

Grayson's jaw tightened. Women were indeed the strangest of creatures. Why she would allow herself to be dressed in something that did not fit unless she wore a contraption that left her unable to breathe was a mystery. "Absolutely not. You could not breathe," Grayson growled.

"Breathing is overrated, my lord. I would rather be in a full swoon and carried out of the house like a sack of potatoes than be seen like this."

He thought about it for a minute as he studied her worried countenance. To have Addie's virtue called into question if she returned in a loosened gown after being gone for a noticeable amount of time with him was not the best thing to do.

"All right. This is what we will do. I will re-fasten your stays and gown, but not as tight as your maid had it."

"The gown won't close otherwise," Addie moaned.

Grayson was torn between howling in frustration and laughing uproariously at his predicament. All the years he'd played the rogue before he married Margaret had not taught him how to deal with this mess. He'd undone and done up numerous gowns very quickly in every sort of situation one could think of. Except this.

But it was up to him to get them out of the house without ruining Addie's reputation. "Yes, the blasted gown will close. I assure you. Certainly well enough to get us out of the ball-room and back into my carriage. It is quite crowded, and despite the hundreds of candles, the lighting is not bright. I will merely walk very close behind you so no one can see the back of your gown that well."

Addie sighed. "That will appear quite strange, but I don't see as we have any other choice. She slid his jacket off her shoulders and handed it to him. He shrugged into the garment and twirled his finger in the air to indicate she should turn around.

Touching her warm, soft skin did strange things to his lower parts. His cock immediately began to show interest in the proceedings and seemed prepared to come out and play.

He chastised himself for his salacious thoughts as he did his best to get the gown fastened enough for propriety's sake, but with enough room for the poor woman to breathe.

He bent close to her ear as he worked the last fastener of the gown. "Promise me you will toss this garment into the trash the minute your maid removes it from you,"

Addie gasped and glanced over her shoulder. "I could never do that. Mother would be outraged!"

"The gown doesn't fit," he growled.

She sighed. "Mother always ordered my gowns too small, hoping by the time they were finished I would have lost enough inches to fit into it."

He stared at her. "That's absurd. Why would she think you need to lose inches?"

Addie opened her mouth to speak, then closed it, then opened it again. "Because I am not as slender as other girls."

He shook his head in disgust. Here was a woman with a perfectly acceptable, curvy, lush body, and her mother wanted her to fit into something smaller. He would never understand women. "You are not as tall as some ladies, either. Does she have plans to stretch you on a rack?"

Despite the pained expression Addie had been wrestling with, she burst out laughing. Not one of those titters or giggles that other ladies were so fond of doing. An honest to goodness laugh. It made him laugh, and he pulled her in for another kiss.

"Here they are!" Lady Stratford, a very attractive and recently widowed lady, who had made suggestions to him earlier, walked into the library with Lady Stevenson and Lady Diana on her heels. The three women watched them, a growing expression of horror, mixed with delight, on their faces at catching them in the dark room in each other's arms.

And they hadn't yet seen the back of Addie's gown.

Nothing to be done for it. Grayson placed his hand at Addie's waist and pulled her close. He could feel her heart pounding against his side, and worried that she would now actually swoon.

Propping her up, he said, "Ladies, how very thoughtful of you to search for us. I'm afraid you've caught Miss Mallory and myself as we were celebrating. She has just made me the happiest of men and consented to be my wife. I hope you will wish us happy."

One of the women squeaked.

At least Addie didn't faint in his arms.

## 11

"OH MY GOODNESS. WHAT A SURPRISE," LADY STEVENSON narrowed her eyes. "I hadn't realized you even knew each other."

Surprise? Despite the horror of the situation, Addie almost laughed at Lady Stevenson's words since she had seen them arrive together. The woman had whisked Grayson away so quickly to meet her niece that she'd almost run him into the wall.

Addie would call the situation more shock than surprise. She felt as though she was in a play where everyone knew their lines except her. *Damn*—the situation called for strong language—she didn't even know if she should laugh or cry.

Or possibly swoon.

In less than a few seconds, more people joined them at the door to the library. "What's this?" Lord Stevenson moved past the three ladies still blocking the doorway and lit two of the gas lamps on the large wooden desk, casting light onto the tableau.

Grayson straightened his shoulders. "I'm afraid Lady Stevenson, Lady Stratford, and Lady Diana happened upon my betrothed, and I just as she accepted my hand in marriage."

"You don't say," the man declared with a huge smile. "That is truly good news, young man." He turned to a footman who had joined the group. "Let's have a toast to the newly betrothed couple. I believe champagne is in order."

Celebrate? Addie felt as though the remains of her last meal was about to make a reappearance at her feet. She stood, only half-dressed, in front of all these people who had rejected her so many times during her Seasons, and Grayson, who had just casually announced their engagement as if he did this sort of thing every day.

Whatever had possessed him? Not being a stupid woman, and well aware of the workings of Society, she knew that being found together in a dark room would cast dispersions on her reputation. But for Grayson to quickly make that announcement rattled her to her very bones.

They didn't live in London. They would be back at home in Bath in a matter of days. Did it truly matter if her sterling reputation was smudged? Being a spinster and store owner wasn't exactly the epitome of *ton*. What was one more mark against her?

Grayson bowed. "Thank you, my lord. That is very kind; however, my fiancée is not feeling well, and I believe she wishes to return home."

It appeared their plan to casually stroll out of the ball with Grayson covering her back was not going to work. "In fact, she is suffering from chills right now." He quickly removed his jacket once again and placed it over Addie's shoulders.

"Oh, that's too bad." Lady Stevenson eyed her with concern. Or was it suspicion? "Most likely, all the excitement."

Grayson nudged Addie. She hadn't said a word since they were stumbled upon.

She jerked. "Yes, my lady. I'm afraid the excitement was too much for me." She offered a weak smile, quelling the urge to place the back of her hand on her forehead and sigh with maidenly air. Lord knew her knees were having trouble holding her up, and her heart pounded so fiercely she was growing lightheaded again.

"I must agree that Miss Mallory does look a bit peaked," Lady Stevenson said with a smirk. Well then. Yes, let us get in some nasty words before the disgraced couple left.

Grayson placed his hand on her lower back and moved her forward. "I wish you all a good evening and hope you enjoy the rest of the ball. We will be leaving now." He turned to the footman who was still waiting for instructions about the champagne. "Will you see that my carriage is brought around?"

The crowd separated like the Red Sea as Addie and Grayson moved toward the door. She could feel the eyes of the ladies in the room burning a hole in the back of Grayson's jacket.

She should have known better than to go to a London ball. They never turned out well for her. Of course, getting engaged had never been one of the things she'd worried about before tonight.

They both remained silent as they waited for the carriage to arrive. Grayson deftly switched his jacket for her full-length wool cape when the footman presented her with it.

Addie's fingers clutched the high neck collar of the cape, rubbing the soft wool against her cheeks, trying her best to cover every inch of her body. She felt as though everyone in the ballroom could see the back of her gown, even though that was impossible. More than anything, she wanted to be home in Bath, in her cozy house with no condemning eyes staring at her.

Once she and Grayson were settled in his carriage, he tapped on the ceiling to have the driver move forward. The jerky motion of the carriage soon smoothed out over the cobblestones.

He leaned across the space separating them and took her hand. "I am sorry for what happened tonight. Not sorry I kissed you, but sorry we were stumbled upon."

"I agree." Addie's voice shook. She was shivering, unable to control herself. Even though the air was a bit chilly, her shaking was more from nerves than anything else. The entire matter was now just sinking in, forcing her to think about her future life.

"Come here." Grayson tugged her forward until she was sitting next to him. He reached under the seat and pulled out a wool blanket that he wrapped around her shoulders, then pulled her close to his side.

The warmth radiating from his body, contained by the blanket, began to ease her shivers. "What are we going to do?" she asked, once her teeth stopped chattering.

"Well, it appears the next step will be to meet with your father and work out the marriage settlements."

Addie sighed. "I was afraid you were going to say that." She turned so she could look into his face. "We don't live in London. We live in Bath. No one there will care that we were caught in the Stevenson's library."

He peered down at her, the amusement in his eyes visible from the lantern alongside the wall of the carriage. "Your reputation is at risk here, Addie. No matter where we live, the scandal will follow. And what of your parents? Do you think your father will allow this to pass?

"Do you believe your mother won't be planning the wedding breakfast the minute one of her cohorts calls on her tomorrow to tell them of tonight's titillating saga? And you can count on any number of women arriving for tea tomorrow."

Addie slumped. "You are right."

Grayson placed his knuckle under her chin and lifted her head. "Is marriage to me so very off-putting?" Even though his tone was light, the quick flash of pain in his eyes startled her. In fact, it was so quick she wasn't quite sure she'd seen it.

"No. I think we might get on fairly well. I already love Michael." The question was, of course, could she love Michael's father? Did she want to? When she was younger, before the experience of the marriage mart had dampened her enthusiasm for the married state, she had expected to fall in love with the man she married.

She believed in romance and expected to live happily ever after with her chosen spouse. They would have a nursery full of children, laugh a great deal, and grow old together. Then reality set in. Seeing so many unhappy couples and numerous spouses switching beds after a short period of time, she'd grown cynical.

Were all marriages like that? Her parents' marriage was certainly not full of passion and love, but she was as certain as one could be that neither one of them had been unfaithful.

There were many things about Grayson that appealed to her. He was a loving and caring father, he was handsome, and he made her shiver inside when he kissed her. Even if the last kiss ended in disaster.

"And Michael already loves you," Grayson said in response to her statement.


GRAYSON CONSIDERED HIS WORDS. HIS SON HAD INDEED developed a strong attachment to Addie. He had no doubt that she would be a good mother to the boy. He snorted, thinking she would be a much better one than the woman who had given him life.

But what about Addie as a wife? As his wife?

He had no doubt that bedding her would be a delight. Truth be told, his hands itched to run over those curves and feel her soft skin. He could just imagine her plump breasts, wide hips, and well-rounded buttocks. When it came to Miss Addie Mallory, there was a lot for a man to enjoy.

The couple of kisses they'd shared told him there was passion in her just waiting to be unleashed, and he was the man to do it. His biggest concern was the fear of caring too much.

It was not a long ride to the Mallory townhouse, and Grayson was determined to do this proposal business the right way. It was what Addie deserved. He tapped on the ceiling of the coach and instructed the driver to keep driving until he told him to stop.

Addie looked at him, her brows raised. "What are you doing?"

Grayson turned so he faced her. She looked so forlorn, buried as she was in her wool coat pulled high on her chin with the blanket surrounding her. Like a lost waif. All he could see were her eyes, but at least she had stopped shaking.

"I'm sorry that you were forced into this engagement, but I must tell you I am not at all sorry." He smiled when she opened her mouth to form a circle and frowned.

"I believe, given enough time, I would have proposed marriage to you eventually. We do get along quite well, and you are everything any man could want in a wife."

She snorted but didn't say anything.

He slid to one knee and fumbled in the blanket to take both her hands in his. Even though she no longer shook, her hands remained cold as ice. He could feel it even with both of them wearing gloves.

"Miss Mallory, would you do me the great honor of consenting to be my wife? Not because we have to, but because I want and desire you, and I hope you would want to freely accept me as your husband."

She hesitated so long he thought she would say no, that she preferred disgrace to marriage with him. Given the way his last marriage went on, he would not be surprised. Perhaps he was simply not a marital prize.

But a slow smile spread over her face, and she nodded. "Yes. I accept your proposal, my lord."

He surprised himself at the sense of relief that raced through his body. When had he decided that marriage with Addie was right? But it was. It felt right, even more so than when he proposed to Margaret.

That was a good sign.

"I believe a kiss is in order." He wrapped her in his arms and pulled her close. She eagerly parted her lips for him, and his tongue swept in, touching all the sensitive parts of her mouth. The slight moan coming from her raised the temperature in his body. Yes, this was a good decision. They would have friendship and passion. That was enough for him.

*But is it enough for Addie?*

THE NEXT MORNING, GRAYSON STOOD ON THE TOP STEP OF THE Mallory townhouse, straightened his ascot, and pulled on his jacket sleeves before dropping the comical knocker on the front door. When he left Addie the night before, she had indicated that she would wait for him to speak to her father before telling her parents about their betrothal.

Grayson had sent around a note asking for a time to speak with Mr. Mallory. He hoped to come early enough so that Mrs. Mallory would not have already been inundated with friends who had attended the Stevenson ball the night before and were quite anxious to relate the tale of Addie's fall from grace.

He dropped the knocker, and the door was immediately opened by the butler. He opened his mouth to speak just as Mrs. Mallory came bustling down the corridor, with her arms extended. "My dear, dear Lord Berkshire. How very, very pleased Mr. Mallory and I are to see you."

Apparently, the gossips of London had reached Mrs.

Mallory before he did. They must have risen at dawn to do their dirty work. He sighed and accepted her embrace. "Good morning, Mrs. Mallory."

She took him by the arm, and beaming brightly, walked him back the way she had come, chatting the entire time about some sort of household matter she needed to attend to first thing that morning.

Apparently, since he was soon to be a member of the family, Mrs. Mallory's household matters were open for discussion. They went into the library where Mr. Mallory was just rising from behind his desk. "Lord Berkshire. How very pleasant to see you." He rushed forward and shook his hand. At least he didn't try to hug him.

He found himself getting annoyed on Addie's behalf. These two were acting as though a proposal for their daughter was so unexpected that they found themselves dancing on air.

"It is pleasant to see you as well, Mr. Mallory."

"Please have a seat." Mr. Mallory waved to the comfortable blue and white striped chair in a semi-circular arrangement in front of the fireplace.

"I have sent for tea, but if you would care for breakfast, it would not take Cook long to whip something up for you." Mrs. Mallory continued to beam at him, all of them still standing because he would not sit while she stood.

"No, thank you. I've broken my fast, but tea is always welcomed."

Since no one said anything, and they all just stood staring at each other, Grayson decided to take the bull by the horns. "I would like to speak with you, Mr. Mallory, and you as well, Mrs. Mallory, about your daughter."

It didn't seem possible, but Mrs. Mallory's smile grew brighter. Good grief, was this what Addie had lived with for years? No wonder she had escaped to Bath.

"Of course." Mrs. Mallory took a seat. Finally, he could sit down. He had brought the usual documents with him to assure Addie's parents that she would we well provided for. He also brought letters of recommendation from his man of business, as well as his solicitor, personal friend, and business partner, Mr. Carter Westbrooke, who could attest to Grayson's sobriety, loyalty, and responsibility.

He had need of these when he negotiated with the bank for the money to buy his last factory. As soon as they were finished here, he would visit with a solicitor he oftentimes used in London and have him draw up the contracts. He needed all of this done quickly.

Before they started, the door to the library opened, and a footman rolled in a tea cart. They chatted about the weather—of course—Parliament's latest antics—of course—the poor condition of the roads in London—of course—and the plans already in the making for the queen's golden jubilee—of course. All subjects well-mannered Brits used for small talk when an important matter was looming on the horizon.

After tea and a selection of tarts and biscuits had been consumed, Mrs. Mallory wiped her mouth on a napkin and placed it next to her empty teacup. She stood, both men following suit. "I will leave you to your discussion."

Grayson breathed a sigh of relief. He wasn't sure why, but he felt uncomfortable with the idea of Mrs. Mallory being part of the meeting. He was sure the woman had plenty to occupy her time with the upcoming wedding, which he planned to tell Addie would be sooner rather than later.

He had received a notice in the mail that very morning from the barrister he'd employed that the court hearing on the competency of Michael was in four weeks. That gave them time for a quick wedding and a very short wedding trip. He also had to make sure that Michael was learning sign language.

They had found a tutor for him, but given the current circumstances, they would not return to Bath until the hearing was over. The tutor would begin working with

Michael, Mrs. Banfield, and Addie immediately. This would be a very trying time for all of them.

His meanderings were interrupted by Mr. Mallory. Once the door closed on Mrs. Mallory, the man rubbed his hands together and said, "So, let's get down to business, eh?"

## 12

ADDIE STARED AT HERSELF IN THE MIRROR WITH ASTONISHMENT. She looked like a bride! Something she had quite given up on a few years ago.

The virginal white gown and veil didn't look so bad after all. Addie would have preferred a nice new gown in a lovely blue or rose that she could use for formal affairs with her new husband. *Husband.*

She gulped.

She and Mother had argued over just about everything having to do with the wedding. Addie's newly acquired confidence from being on her own and making her own decisions as a successful businesswoman gave her the courage to do something she'd never done before, and that was to go against Mother's wishes.

It started with announcing that she and Grayson wished to be married as soon as possible. Mother was appalled, even though she had heard from numerous sources that her daughter was on the brink of ruination.

"I don't agree with this, Adeline. If you have a rushed wedding, gossip will start up again, and everyone will be watching your waistline for months." Mother threatened.

Addie sighed and continued to lick the envelopes for the select fifty or so invitations to the wedding breakfast that Mother had written out. "Mother, the gossip is already there and will continue until the next scandal erupts. Lord Berkshire has a very good reason for a quick wedding." At her mother's raised eyebrows, Addie blushed. "No. Not that. He has a legal issue with his son that he must concentrate on."

Mother sniffed and crossed another name off the list as Addie handed her the envelope. "Nothing should be more important than a man's wedding."

"His son is very important to him. And I think as a good, responsible father, he made the correct decision." Addie didn't add that she also wanted the whole thing over with as quickly as possible. Never having been the center of attention, she found she did not enjoy the idea of everyone watching her every move. Lord knew her moves were clumsy at best.

Addie's thoughts came back to the vision of herself in the mirror. She had made some concessions to her mother and had agreed to keep her somewhat happy by wearing the newly traditional white wedding gown and veil, even though at her age she felt ridiculous. Some compromises needed to be made, and she could live with this one.

"Oh, my, you look beautiful," Lottie gushed as she and Pamela burst into her room. Her friends had arrived two days before, and they'd spent as much time as possible catching up on things Addie had missed in her time away. The women were fortunate enough to find someone they trusted to mind the bookstore while they traveled to London and attended the wedding.

"I look like a bride." Addie smirked.

"Yes. And that is what you are. Who would ever have guessed when Lord Berkshire walked into your bookstore that morning, he would end up your husband?" Lottie shook her head.

"I am sure stranger things have been recorded throughout

time." Addie adjusted the top of her veil, containing fresh flowers that Mother must have had a devil of a time finding at this time of the year.

Lottie had declined acting as a bridesmaid, not wanting to call attention to herself. Which was utterly impossible, since Lottie was the most beautiful woman Addie had ever seen. But she'd noticed a distinct sense of unease in her friend from the moment she had arrived in London.

Lottie had once confessed to Addie and Pamela that her mother was well-known in London, and they'd had terrible falling out before Lottie had quit London to take up residency in Bath.

Pamela would act as her witness and bridesmaid, and Grayson had asked Mr. Carter Westbrooke, his solicitor from Bath and a close friend, to act as his witness.

"Adeline, it's time to leave for the church, dear." Mother entered her room, studying her hands as she pulled on her gloves. She looked up and came to an abrupt halt. To Addie's dismay, tears filled Mother's eyes. "Oh, my."

Addie felt her own eyes moisten and prayed she could pull herself together and not arrive at the church with a blotchy face. "Oh, Mother, please don't."

They crossed the room toward each other and embraced. "You are a beautiful bride, Adeline." Mother leaned back and looked at her. "And a wonderful daughter. Be happy, my dear."

By now, all four women were patting the corners of their eyes. "Enough of this," Lottie said, waving her hand around. "I believe it is time to leave for the church."

Mother had fallen in love with Lottie and Pamela as much as Addie had. In fact, her mother had told her at breakfast a couple of days before that if she knew Addie had such good friends in Bath, she would not have worried about her so much.

Of course, Mother's next question about her friends had been to ask why they were not seeking husbands. Addie dodged that question by suggesting they could use another pot of tea, and quickly left the room to fetch it from the kitchen.

The four women made their way downstairs, where Father and Addie's brother, Marcus, waited to escort the ladies to the church.

"What a bevy of beauties," Marcus said as he made his bow to the ladies.

"Indeed." Father's face glowed with happiness, which made Addie proud.

They all trooped down to the two carriages to carry them to the church. Grayson had loaned them his rented carriage, so they could all travel at the same time to St. Paul's Cathedral, where the wedding would take place.

Mother, Father, and Addie took one carriage. Lottie, Pamela, and Marcus the other. Marcus had been quite the host since her friends had arrived: joking, teasing, and flirting with them. She felt it necessary, however, to warn them that Marcus had managed to dodge the parson's noose for years, and she had no reason to believe he was ready to succumb anytime soon.

Of course, both girls waved her off with assurances that they had no intention of pursuing her brother. Or any other man for that matter.

Only a handful of friends had been invited to the ceremony with another fifty guests to join in the celebration at the wedding breakfast to follow at the Mallory townhouse.

Mother would have liked to double the number of guests at her only daughter's wedding, but there was simply not enough time to plan for a wedding breakfast of that magnitude in the short time allotted for the preparations.

Addie was hit with a wave of panic as they drew up to the church. Her hand felt damp under her gloves, and her stomach cramped. This was it. What she'd wanted as a young girl and decided she would never have as a young lady.

How well did she even know Lord Berkshire? Since their hurried betrothal, they'd spent very little time together and almost no time alone. He arrived the day after his meeting with Father, with a beautiful opal and diamond ring that had been in his family for years.

He had been careful to assure her that it had not been worn by his deceased wife. It stung that he'd been remarkably silent on that subject. Did he not trust her with that part of his life? The little she knew she'd heard from gossip: that his wife had died under scandalous circumstances. Being an unmarried lady, she was not privy to what those scandalous circumstances had been.

He was a good man. That much she knew. Did she love him? Probably not, but there was a very good chance she would. She doubted if he loved her, but hopefully love would grow there, too. From what she'd seen so far, they certainly shared passion. That was one part of her upcoming nuptials that she had to admit she was anticipating.

Also, in just a matter of minutes, she would be a mother. Something she'd always wanted. That part was exciting. Despite all the frenzy about the wedding she had managed to spend as much time as possible with Michael and the tutor, Mr. Graves, learning sign language. The boy was progressing remarkably fast, and Mr. Graves told her that her word blindness—which he said had now been termed 'dyslexia'— actually made her a good candidate for sign language.

Her mind back to the matter at hand, she took a deep breath as Pamela shook out the back of her gown, and the organist began to play. Father stepped up to her, and after giving her a kiss on the cheek, placed her hand on his arm, and they began the walk down the aisle.

She immediately spotted Grayson standing next to who she assumed was his friend, Mr. Westbrooke. Since he hadn't been due to arrive until this morning, she had not yet met him. Her knees were shaky, and she was grateful to have Father's arm to hold onto.

Was she doing the right thing? Should she abscond back to Bath and take up her comfortable life?

They reached the sanctuary, and she looked into Grayson's deep brown eyes as he looked back at her. His crooked smile did strange things to her insides. He was so handsome it hurt her eyes to look at him.

Her groom's wedding attire fit his large body perfectly, and his hair, although slicked back for the occasion, had already begun to settle on his forehead. She licked her lips and leaned in as Father kissed her and then handed her off to Grayson.

He squeezed her hand. "Relax, sweetheart. It will be over soon."

"I am afraid not, my lord. This is just the beginning."


GRAYSON TOOK ADDIE'S HAND IN HIS, AND THEY TURNED TO face the vicar. He tried not to think about the last time he'd done this very same thing and it had ended so badly. After Margaret's death, he swore he would never do it again, but here he stood.

However, comparing Margaret with Addie was more than foolish. Margaret had been all things evil. Things he'd never seen in her when they were courting and first married. Love had blinded him to her vain, selfish nature. In her eyes, nothing came before her wishes and desires. Not even her baby son.

Addie, on the other hand, was a loving, caring person, and he knew in his heart she would never betray her marriage vows.

The actual ceremony seemed to be over rather quickly. He spoke clearly the words that would bind him to Addie for life and then slid a wedding band on her finger. He gave her the expected chaste kiss, and they turned to face the friends and family gathered in the church.

It was done. He had a wife again. God help him.

LATER THAT EVENING, GRAYSON PACED THE SOFT, DEEP BROWN carpet in his bedchamber, waiting for word from the newly hired lady's maid that Addie was ready for him. They were spending their wedding night at his townhouse, and in the morning, they would leave by train for a short wedding trip to Brighton Beach. Michael was in good hands with Mrs. Banfield, and Mrs. Mallory had already taken on her role as grandmother and been delighted to learn a little bit of sign language herself.

Grayson ran his fingers through his hair and admitted he was anxious to bed his new wife. The bit of passion he'd felt in her when they'd kissed had stirred him in a way that he hadn't felt since he and Margaret were first married.

Truth be told, even Margaret had not brought him to the edge of losing control as Addie had the few times they'd kissed.

There was something about the voluptuousness of her body compared to Margaret's slender form that appealed to him in a way he'd never expected.

"My lord, Lady Berkshire is ready." The demure young maid gave a quick bob and fled, her face red. Ah, the innocence of youth.

He tightened the belt on his banyan and entered the sitting room separating the two bedchambers. He gave a slight knock and entered Addie's room.

He realized that they'd not even had enough time together since their betrothal to discuss where she would sleep. He much preferred to have his wife by his side all night, but Margaret had been adamant that she could never enjoy a good night's sleep with him tossing and turning next to her.

Whenever they made love—in his room—she would quickly dress and hurry away. Since his parents had a stilted relationship and to his knowledge never shared a room, he didn't find that so unusual. Since then, he'd made friends with men who eschewed the 'sleep apart' nonsense, and he hoped he could convince his new wife of the benefits of that.

One benefit, of course, was knowing who was occupying one's wife's bed.

Addie stood before the fireplace, bringing his thoughts and movements to an abrupt halt. She was achingly beautiful. Her silky hair flowed over her shoulders and ended right at her full breasts. She wore a deep rose satin nightgown that clung to her curves in a scandalous manner. It was cut low, with only two narrow bands of fabric over her shoulders holding the entire thing up.

"My mother picked out my nightgown."

Grayson slowly walked toward her. "Remind me to buy her a dozen roses and a very expensive bracelet."

"You like it?" She looked as if she wasn't sure, which only convinced him the woman did not own a mirror.

"Oh, yes. Yes, indeed." His steady continuous advance caused her to back up.

He reached his hand out. "Stop, sweetheart. If you get any closer to the fireplace, we will spend our wedding night at London Hospital."

Addie chewed on her lip and took his outstretched hand.

"Come here." He gave her a slight tug then wrapped his arms around her waist and pulled her to his chest. "Are you frightened?"

She tilted her head and studied him. "No. Not exactly. Curious, certainly. Well, maybe a bit nervous."

"I had a bottle of wine brought up earlier. Would you care for a glass? It might relax you."

She shook her head, and then to his amazement, wrapped her hand around the back of his head and pulled him down to meet her lips. If Addie was indeed a bit nervous, it did not show in the way she enthusiastically, albeit innocently, devoured his mouth.

Not wanting to deter her, he allowed her the freedom to explore his mouth, her soft tongue tentatively touching his, then moving to reach further inside his mouth. Her lack of experience, along with her eagerness, stirred him more than any mistress or courtesan ever could.

It became obvious she didn't know where to go from there, so he took over, pulling her close, feeling the warmth and softness of her breasts pressed up against his chest.

Her heart beat a thunderous rhythm against his body, and slight moans came from her as he plundered her mouth. Grayson pulled away and scattered kisses over her jaw, behind her ear and down to the tops of her magnificent breasts. He slid the two thin straps over her shoulders and moved back to watch the satin slide slowly down her body, revealing inch by inch what he'd been dreaming about for weeks.

She was magnificent. A goddess waiting for her subjects to worship at her feet. Every inch of creamy skin was there for the taking. "Damnation, you are beautiful. I could stare at you all night and never get enough."

A slow blush crept up her body from her soft middle all the way to her face. "I'm not comfortable with you staring at me."

"Oh, darling, you better get used to it. I could gaze at you for days." She was soft in all the places where he was hard. She had full, magnificent breasts with pouty pink nipples. Her slightly rounded belly, full plump bottom, and strong legs that he couldn't wait to feel wrapped around him drove every single drop of blood in his body to his cock.

He bent her over his arm, giving him access to her breasts, which he suckled, teasing their peaks into hardness with his tongue.

"Shouldn't you be undressed, too?" Her raspy, breathless voice stirred him into action.

"Indeed, I should and shall." He picked her up and walked to the large, comfortable bed in the middle of the room, dropping her so she bounced. And giggled.

Before he could loosen his belt, she rose up on her knees and stopped his movement. "Let me."

Yes. This virtuous wife of his had a wanton streak in her that he planned to encourage. She studied his face, her eyelids heavy and a satisfied smirk on her lips, as she undid the belt to his banyan and opened the flaps to push the garment off his shoulders, leaving him as bare as she.

She ran her palms over his chest, stopping to rub his flat nipples with her thumbs. He sucked in air between his teeth and closed his eyes. She was going to kill him. He wanted nothing more than to push her back onto the bed and thrust his aching cock into her until she screamed with pleasure.

But this was her wedding night, and she was a virgin. He wanted it to be as pleasurable for her as possible since this could very well set the tone for the rest of their marriage.

Slowly, he eased her onto her back and rested on the bed alongside her, partially covering her with his body. "I want you to enjoy this. I assume your mother has told you what would happen tonight?"

"Yes. And I pray she was wrong."

A soft smile played at his lips. "Why?"

"Because she told me it was not very pleasant, but it was my 'duty' so I should lay back and—"

"Think of England," he finished.

They both laughed.

"I don't want you to think about anything except us, our hands and mouths, and the pleasure we will give each other."

She grinned. "I'm ready."

He pushed back the hair that had fallen on her forehead. "Oh, yes, my love. And so am I."

## 13

A WEEK AFTER THE WEDDING, AND A VERY RAMBUNCTIOUS AND pleasurable wedding trip, Addie and Grayson returned to his London townhouse, both of them anxious to see Michael.

Addie was amazed at how well she'd taken to marriage and to the marriage bed. They'd spent more time in bed than they did taking in the sights in Brighton Beach. Because it was well into autumn, they couldn't partake of the waters anyway, but that only gave them more of an excuse to remain indoors.

In bed.

So far, marriage had been wonderful. Grayson was a thoughtful and considerate man, who treated her well, constantly asking after her welfare. They dined in the best restaurants, strolled along the beach, and eventually ended up in bed wrapped in each other's arms.

Now she was ready to assume her position as Countess of Berkshire. Getting through the court hearing for Michael and making sure she could communicate with the boy effectively was the priority upon their return. Grayson had learned some sign language, but she had picked it up much faster, even more so than Mrs. Banfield.

Once the hearing was over, they would return to Bath.

Addie was anxious to see how her store had fared in her absence. There would be much for her to do with the upcoming Christmas season, when the prior owner, Mr. Evans, had told her she could expect a great many sales.

Even though Mr. Dickens' book, *A Christmas Carol*, was published over forty years before, Mr. Evans assured her she would receive many requests for a copy once December arrived.

She was excited to decorate her store for Christmas, too. She could already see the cute little toys and books she would display in the front window.

Excitedly, she turned to Grayson as his rented carriage transporting them from the train to his townhouse pulled away from the station. "I put an order in for my Christmas books over a month ago. I should dash off a note to Lottie and make sure they arrived."

Grayson waved his hand. "Do not fret over that, sweeting. Let the new owner deal with any problems having to do with book orders." He looked out the window at the cloudy day. "I hope the rain holds off until we've unloaded all of our luggage." He grinned at her. "You certainly bought enough things on our trip."

Addie had frozen at his words. She shook her head as if she could loosen the words her new husband had just spoken. "What did you say?"

He reached out and ran his finger down her cheek. "I said, my dear, you purchased enough things in Brighton Beach to fill up the entire newly added suitcase."

Her hands fisted in her lap, and her heart thudding like a racehorse, she took a deep breath. "No. That's not what I meant. I'm asking what you said about my bookstore?"

He regarded her with raised brows. "I said it was not necessary for you to fret about the bookstore since the new owner will deal with any issues that arose while you were gone. I have two potential buyers interested in purchasing the shop."

Addie felt closer to swooning than she had when she had worn the tightened stays that had landed her in this position. Married to a man who now assumed he would run her life.

She raised her chin. "I am sorry you have gone through such trouble, my lord, because I have no intention of selling *my* bookstore."

Grayson took one final look out the window and dropped the curtain. "It will be much easier on you to have a new owner than to try to hire someone competent to run the place."

"Wait." She put her shaking hand up to stop him. "I believe we are at a crossroads here, my lord. I have no intention of selling my store, nor having someone run it for me. It is *my* store. I own it. I shall run it."

The man actually looked surprised. No. He looked aghast. "You will not be working in a bookstore."

"Not *a* bookstore, *my lord*. *My* bookstore."

All humor and teasing left his voice and demeanor. "I will not have my countess working in a store like a common laborer. You have a proper place to assume in Society, the management of my households, looking out for the welfare of my tenants, and the care of my son.

She gritted her teeth. "*My* household. *My* tenants. *My* son. Do you not see anything wrong with that?"

The blasted dimwit actually looked confused. "No. What is wrong with what I said?"

Addie wanted to punch someone in the face. Not just someone, but her new husband. However, since the carriage was drawing up to the front of the townhouse, she managed to get herself under control. Barely. "We will discuss this later."

She would not show up at her new home, screaming like a shew for all the servants and neighbors to witness. She would be dignified and graceful. She would enter the townhouse as the lady she was. She would meet the staff and then suggest they send for tea. She would drink it and eat lovely biscuits and offer charming chatter.

Then she would invite her cretin husband to their bedchamber. Not for a rousing session in bed, but for a sword-less battle. Maybe not sword-less if she could find one in his house.

The door to the carriage promptly opened, and a footman stood there. "Good afternoon, my lord, my lady." He gave a deep bow.

"Good afternoon, Jason." Grayson jumped from the carriage and turned to assist Addie out. Drawing on all her years of training, she smiled at the footman. "Good afternoon." Then she accepted her husband's hand and promptly exited the carriage landing with all her weight on his foot.

Grayson winced but said nothing.

The childish action making her feel a bit better, Addie walked up the steps, her hand resting on her husband's arm. Because of the chilly weather, the staff was lined up in the corridor, rather than outside, to meet the new lady of the house. Since Grayson was rarely in London, the servants were few.

As she stepped into the entrance hall, Addie cringed at the reminder of the garish decor that she would be more than happy to replace.

The servants smiled, curtsied, and bowed. She put aside her angst at her husband and greeted each staff member warmly, using each one's name as they were introduced to her to help her remember.

That requisite formality out of the way, Addie did as she planned and asked for tea. She made a point of sending for Cook so she could rave about the biscuits, scones, and tarts. The woman was blushing with happiness when she left them.

Addie and her new husband conducted a stilted conversation over tea, exclaiming over the array of treats Cook had sent, the weather, Parliament, the poor conditions of the roads in London, and the plans already in the making for the queen's golden jubilee celebration.

Once Addie was sure they covered all the required subjects, she wiped her mouth, placed the napkin carefully next to her plate, and placed her hands demurely in her lap. "I would request you join me in our bedchamber, my lord."

At first, Grayson's eyes lit up, but when he took a better look at her face, he sobered and nodded. "Of course, my dear."

She swept from the room like a queen and made her way upstairs. Once the door to the bedchamber was closed, Addie drew herself up and faced her husband. "I have no intention of giving up my bookstore. You might be my husband, and by law own all that is mine, but this is one thing on which I will not concede."

He started to move forward, most likely to wrap his arms around her, which would start a whole new activity that she was not ready for just yet.

When she held her hand out, palm up, he stopped and said, "We are both tired from the hurried wedding and trip. Also, we need to focus on the hearing next week. I don't think this is something we should discuss right now."

As much as she hated to give up the conversation, he was correct. The two of them squabbling like children while trying to deal with the upcoming legal issue was not wise. She gave him a brisk nod. "I agree. However, I will say one thing. Do not. I repeat, do not even think to sell my bookstore before we've spoken about this."

"Very well. I agree." He reached his hand out. "Is it possible for us to call a truce now?"

Addie's stomach was still in knots. "I don't think that would work right now."

He walked to the bed, sat down, and patted the spot next to him. "Come join me. Just to talk."

She might be a new bride, but she was already aware of

her husband's tactics. The look he cast her almost had her clothes going up in flames.

He offered her that crooked, little-boy smile that always went right to her heart. "I just want to hold you. Rub your back. It will relax you." With his big brown eyes and the hair falling over his forehead, he almost looked penitent, but she knew better. Still, at his words, she felt her muscles relax and her nipples hardening.

He held his hand out again. "Come here, sweetheart."

She should hold onto her anger and dignity and walk right out the door. Instead, she found her feet slowly moving toward the bed. She sighed. When it came to Grayson, she had little resistance.

Damn the man.

After putting herself to rights following their tumble in bed, Addie spent the rest of the day with Michael. Shortly after they sent a note to Mother informing her of their return, her stepson had returned from the Mallory townhouse, along with Mrs. Banfield, where they had resided while Addie and Grayson had been on their trip.

Addie was truly amazed at how quickly her mother had gone from scheming marriage-minded mama to Grandmama. All the rules and regulations that had applied to Addie and Marcus while growing up seemed to have disappeared with Michael.

And of course, being the smart lad that he was, and very much like his father, Michael played right into her hands. His beautiful smile and loving ways got him pretty much anything he wanted.

Grayson had left after their 'truce' to visit with the barrister who would be meeting them in court the following week. She and Michael were in the library, practicing their sign language. Addie was thrilled at how quickly the boy had picked up the skill. He would need years to master the method of communication, but right now, they could hold a short conversation by moving their hands and pointing. It was incredible.

Brooks, the very imposing butler at the Berkshire townhouse, entered the room. "My lady. You have a caller."

Addie looked up at him from where she sat, very undignified, on the floor, with pictures of various items spread out before them. "Who is calling?"

Brooks walked to where she sat, not showing any sort of reaction to the unseemly position in which he'd found the lady of the house. He handed a card to her.

*Mrs. Peter Hartley*

Addie frowned. The name did not seem familiar to her. She hated asking a personal question of the staff, but she also did not want to admit a caller she knew nothing about. "Do you know Mrs. Hartley?"

Brooks lifted his nose in the air, which told her more than what he was about to say. "She is the widow of his lordship's brother, Mr. Peter Hartley."

Oh, goodness. She was a relative. Addie jumped up and began brushing her skirts, then she realized who Mrs. Hartley was. She was Grayson's sister-in-law, who had brought the legal action against Michael. "One more question, Brooks. Does his lordship have any other brothers?"

She couldn't believe that she was married to a man about whom she knew so little, but theirs had been a quick courtship. The only relative who had attended their wedding had been Michael.

"No, my lady. Mr. Peter Hartley was his lordship's only sibling."

This was the woman who had instigated the legal conflict. Addie patted her hair and glanced down at Michael. "Brooks, will you take Michael upstairs to Mrs. Banfield? And then send for tea after you put Mrs. Hartley in the drawing room."

"That is where she is, my lady."

"Very good. Thank you."

As she straightened her clothing and considered going upstairs to change into something a bit more formal, Addie thought about this woman she was about to meet. She apparently loved her son enough to try to legally wrestle away Grayson's son's inheritance and title.

But on the other hand, she had no regard for her nephew, who was in no way an idiot or incompetent. As she made her way to the drawing room, it occurred to her that it was odd that both Mrs. Hartley and Grayson were widowed.

Addie found the woman standing, her arms crossed, staring out the window. When she heard Addie enter, she turned and regarded her. The first words that came into Addie's head were 'ice queen.'

Mrs. Hartley's hair was so blonde it was almost white. She had very little in the way of eyebrows and her lips, like her skin, was insipid. Her eyes were such a pale blue that Addie was forced to look away. "Good afternoon Mrs. Hartley."

The woman viewed Addie with contempt. "Well, it seems you are the new countess."

A bit taken aback by Mrs. Hartley's greeting, she said, "That would be correct. May we sit down?" Addie waved to the small sofa in front of the fireplace.

"I'm not sure. Perhaps I must remain standing while you sit. Isn't that the way it is with a commoner and the aristocracy?"

Addie was stunned. She had never met anyone who disliked her so much on sight. Even the young ladies who had tortured her throughout her Seasons didn't have the amount of hate that spewed from this woman.

"I have ordered tea. If you wish to continue to stand and hold your cup, saucer, and plate in your hand, that is your prerogative." Addie settled herself on the sofa and looked up at the woman.

Slowly Mrs. Hartley lowered herself to the chair opposite

Addie. "Where did you come from? I had no idea that Grayson was courting anyone."

"And you two were so close that he didn't advise you of that? So close that he forgot to invite you to our wedding? Or perhaps you forgot to come?" Addie was becoming more annoyed by the minute. How dare this woman come into her house and speak to her in this manner.

"He'll never love you, you know."

Addie's heart began to thump, and suddenly she wanted to jump up and leave the room. She was afraid this woman was about to tell her something she did not want to hear.

Attempting an indifferent demeanor, she said, "The relationship I have with my husband is of no concern of yours. Might I ask what is the purpose of your visit? If you have come to welcome me into the family, I am afraid your intention falls a bit short."

Mrs. Hartley leaned back and crossed her arms. "Did he tell you his wife Margaret was running away with my husband, who she was having an affair with, when they were killed in a carriage accident?"

Addie lost her breath and felt the blood drain from her face. So that was the scandal involving Grayson's wife that had been bandied about the *ton*.

The clock behind her ticked much louder than normal while Addie composed herself. "I must once again state that our marriage is none of your business or concern." Addie stood. "Now if you will excuse me, I have other matters needing my attention."

Addie moved swiftly, anxious to be gone from the woman's presence. As she reached the door to the drawing room, Mrs. Hartley called out, "He was desperately in love with Margaret. On the day she was buried, he told me he would never marry again because he could never open up his heart to another woman."

Addie turned back, her chin raised. "Things change."

Mrs. Hartley smirked at her. "Has he told you he loved you?" Her smile grew wider. "Ah, yes. I can see by your expression that he has not."

The woman stood and leaned over to pick up her reticule. "He never will, either. Margaret was the love of his life, and that will never change, no matter how hard you try."

Barely keeping herself under control, Addie whispered, "Please leave my home. Now."

Mrs. Hartley strolled toward the door, swinging her reticule. "I am going, *Lady Berkshire*. But remember when he turns to you in your bed at night and takes you in his arms, he is wishing you were Margaret." With those words resounding off the walls, the harridan made her departure.

Addie leaned against the closed door and wrapped her arms around her middle. She felt sick to her stomach. All the joy and happiness she'd experienced at Brighton Beach had dissolved like sugar in hot tea.

Her husband would never love her, and he planned to sell her bookstore.

## 14

----

IT HAD BEEN A LONG WEEK AS THEY ALL WAITED FOR THE COURT hearing at the Court in Chancery. Grayson already knew Addie was upset about his plan to sell the bookstore, but there was something else bothering her. The closeness they shared during their trip to Brighton Beach had disappeared.

Each day he felt Addie pull farther away from him. They continued to make love every night, but something was missing. The passion was still there, but he no longer felt the closeness.

And he missed it. Missed her.

He hadn't changed his mind about having his countess work in a store, but there had to be some sort of compromise they could reach so things could go back to the way they were.

"Are you ready?" Addie joined him in the library, her empty smile bringing his spirits down further.

Grayson picked up the notes he'd been making while he waited for his wife. "Yes. Where is Michael?"

"He's with Mrs. Banfield. They will be down any minute."

"How does he appear? Is he nervous?"

Addie smiled, the warm smile that used to be for him, but now only appeared when she spoke of Michael. He really had to get to the bottom of this once the hearing ended.

"No. In fact, he appears more excited to show off his new skills than nervous."

Grayson walked toward her and took her hands in his. He raised her hands to his mouth and kissed her knuckles. "I want to thank you for all you've done for my son."

Addie pulled away, her eyes shuttered. "'Tis my duty, my lord." She turned and walked to the door, her back straight.

Grayson shook his head. Yes. He would get to the bottom of this. Soon.

The courthouse loomed before them, and he had to admit to twinges of nervousness himself. His barrister, Mr. Daniel Albright met them as they entered the building.

"Are we ready?" the barrister asked as he joined them, his steps jaunty. He turned from Grayson and bowed to Mrs. Banfield and Addie. "Good morning, my lady. Mrs. Banfield."

When Mr. Albright had suggested that Addie do the interpretation during the hearing for Michael instead of his tutor Mr. Graves, Grayson was a bit reluctant, wanting to make sure everything went well. But Mr. Albright was adamant that Addie would garner more support being a woman, the boy's stepmother, and very competent in sign language.

They entered the room in the Court in Chancery, where the hearing was to be held. Grayson nodded briefly to his sister-in-law, Beatrice, and the man sitting alongside her, who he assumed was her legal representative. His nephew, David Hartley, was nowhere to be seen, but perhaps he wasn't needed for this hearing even though their hoped-for outcome would benefit him.

Grayson immediately noticed that with tightened lips, Addie ignored Beatrice striding right past her, although she had never met her before. He was not in the mood to introduce them, so he just herded his group into the chairs facing the front of the room.

He glanced briefly at Beatrice and frowned at the smirk she tossed at Addie, which he found odd. Addie continued to stare straight ahead, but her face had paled. Perhaps she was nervous, too. He reached over and took her hand in his and gave it a slight squeeze.

The hearing began with the magistrate reading aloud the document filed with the court to have Michael declared incompetent. When he finished, the man removed his spectacles and laid the paper down in front of him.

"I see no reason for this hearing since the boy, in this case, is his father's rightful heir, and unless the father is deceased there is no reason to question the heir's competency."

The man sitting alongside Beatrice, who had been introduced to the court as Mr. Wallingham, stood and addressed the magistrate. "Sir, I wish to explain that the young boy, the Viscount Falmouth, has never spoken a word since his birth and is known to grunt to make himself known.

"We have reason to believe he is incompetent, and wish to have Mr. David Hartley, son of the late Mr. Peter Hartley declared as the heir presumptive."

The magistrate peered down at him. "For what purpose? I'm looking over at Lord Berkshire, who seems to be in fine health to me."

"Sir, I am sure you are aware that accidents happen, and illnesses can take one's life very quickly. We wish to have a smooth transition when the time comes." He blushed and added, "Not that we hope for that occasion to be anytime soon."

The magistrate signaled Mr. Wallingham to take his seat. He then looked over at Mr. Albright. "What have you to say in response to this?"

Mr. Albright stood and acknowledged the magistrate. "Sir, young Michael, the Viscount Falmouth, is not incompetent nor an idiot. He is deaf. And as such, until recently was only able to express himself in grunts.

"However, Lord Berkshire has obtained a tutor who taught his son, as well as the lad's stepmother, Lady Berkshire, sign language. We can prove to the court that Michael is not incompetent in any way."

The magistrate continued to stare at Mr. Albright, his brows rising. "That is quite interesting. I have heard of sign language before but never saw it demonstrated. I would like to see an example."

Mr. Albright nodded at Addie, and she stood, taking Michael's hand. She then moved him to the chair alongside the magistrate and turned to the imposing-looking man. "Sir, you may ask anything of Michael. I will then ask him the question, and he will respond."

This was it. Grayson already felt that the magistrate was on their side, but he wanted so badly to prove to the world that his son, while perhaps not perfect, was still intelligent, and able to speak and communicate in his own way.

"Ask the young man how old he is." The magistrate nodded at Michael.

Addie made the correct signs, Michael signed back, and she turned to the magistrate. "Four years."

Mr. Wallingham stood. "Sir. I must, for the record, state my objection to this. They could be doing anything up there with their fingers. Naturally, his stepmother would know the boy's age."

"You may sit, Mr. Wallingham," the magistrate said. He then turned to Addie. "Lady Berkshire, ask the lad to cross the room and pick up the papers on the table in front of his father."

Addie signed furiously. Michael wrinkled his brows. Mr. Wallingham snorted and glanced sideways at a grinning Beatrice. Grayson held his breath, but after about a minute, Michael left his chair, walked over to the table and took the papers in his hand and brought them back to Addie.

She took the papers from him and wrapped her arms

around him, pulling him close. Tears ran down her face, and Grayson felt as though he'd been hit with a bolt of lightning. His insides twisted, and his heart beat faster. A sense of joy filled him like never before in his life.

He loved her.

He loved his wife. His countess. His everything. Why he hadn't realized it before now had only to do with his own stubbornness. His need to cling to the idea that he would never give his heart to another woman.

But this was Addie. Kind, caring, loyal, and faithful Addie, who was so full of honor, she would never betray him the way Margaret had. And their love was not the passion of youthful lust, but the kind of love that lasts a lifetime. He wanted them to be old and gray and holding hands when the first of them left this earth.

Now he was anxious for the hearing to be over so he could tell her how he felt. If she wanted to work in a bookstore, she could work in a bookstore. He never cared too much for what Society thought before, why should he care now when it was so important to the woman he loved?

*The woman I love.*

His heart pounded with excitement.

"Mr. Wallingham, it appears to me that there is nothing wrong or incompetent with the Viscount Falmouth. He is a sweet, charming lad who can communicate with no problems. That shall be my decision, but a formal legal ruling will be sent to all the parties involved." He looked down at Michael and waved. "I might not know sign language, but I believe that is the universal sign for saying goodbye."

Michael smiled and waved back.

The magistrate slammed down his gavel. "This matter is concluded."

They all rose as the magistrate stood and left the room.

As they gathered up their papers, Beatrice strode over to their table. "You might have pulled some tomfoolery here for the court, but I don't believe for one minute that Michael is not an idiot."

Addie stood and addressed Beatrice. "You may rest assured that no one here cares what you believe." Then she turned her back, took Michael's hand, and swept by Beatrice like a queen leaving her lowly subject.

ADDIE'S HEAD WAS POUNDING BY THE TIME THE CARRIAGE reached the townhouse. They had won. She was happy and grateful for that. After a few congratulations among those in the carriage, they had all remained silent for the rest of the trip.

However, while everyone was joyful and excited, nothing had changed for her. She was still married to a man who only wed her because they'd been caught in a compromising situation. He had no intention of ever loving another woman after his beloved Margaret, and if given his way, he would sell the one thing Addie had built for herself without any care for her feelings.

"I will leave you all here," Grayson said, as they exited the carriage. "I must meet with my man of business at my club in preparation for our return to Bath tomorrow."

Addie nodded and entered the house. She handed her cloak off to Brooks and turned to Mrs. Banfield. "If you will excuse me, I think I will lie down. I seem to be suffering from a megrim."

Mrs. Banfield touched her hand lightly. "That is a very good idea, my lady. I am sure you could use the rest now that all the tension from the hearing is over."

Addie nodded and knelt in front of Michael. She signed how proud she was of him and how much she loved him. Then she gave him a hug and kiss, then climbed the stairs to her room to prepare to return to her own house in Bath.

Because she had opted to bring only a few items with her,

not expecting such a lengthy visit, she was able to leave for Bath within the hour of arriving home from the hearing. She'd left a note for Grayson explaining that she was returning to her old life. Yes, they were married and would remain married, but it had been a mistake.

Since she had given up on ever having a husband, and he was still madly in love with his Margaret, there was no reason to pretend they wanted to stay married. They had staved off the gossipers with their quick betrothal and wedding and saved his son from losing his inheritance.

She loved Michael with her whole heart and would make sure she stayed in his life. He would be the only child she ever had, and her the only mother he would ever know.

The sad part was how much she loved Grayson, something she'd begun to realize right before the disastrous visit from Mrs. Hartley.

On the way home from Brighton Beach, she had been filled with love and joy at how wise their decision to marry had been. During the short wedding trip, they had shared intimate dinners in their hotel room, feeding each other from their forks, drinking wine that spilled down her front, forcing a laughing Grayson to lay her back on the thick carpet and lick it off.

They'd made love so many times she didn't think she could walk. He read to her while sitting naked on the floor in front of the fireplace. Not once had he criticized her for not being able to read out loud to him.

It had been a wonderful time, and even though things had not turned out the way she hoped, the memories would keep her warm on the cold nights alone in her bed. As long as she could stop crying.

Love was not supposed to hurt. But this did. Tremendously. So bad was the pain that she wanted to wrap her arms around her middle and curl up into a ball of misery. But life must go on, and her business needed her. She'd been very happy before Lord Berkshire had walked into her store and her life. She would be again.

Alfred Tennyson said, "'Tis better to have loved and lost than never to have loved at all." Although she agreed with the adage at the time she'd read it, now that she'd experienced love, she wasn't so sure Tennyson was as brilliant as she'd thought.

By the time she reached the Bath Spa train station, she was exhausted, tired of crying, and determined to claim her life back. She hired a hackney to return her home.

She walked into the small house she loved so much and didn't feel the rising sense of happiness it always had given her. But then, she left the house with the idea of going to London to help Grayson find a tutor for Michael.

She returned an unwanted and unloved bride. With those somber thoughts, she climbed the stairs to her bedchamber and collapsed on the bed, falling into a dead sleep.

"WHAT DO YOU MEAN SHE'S GONE?" GRAYSON HANDED HIS COAT off to Brooks. He'd just returned from his meeting, which had gone very well, and now was ready to speak with Addie and get to the bottom of whatever it was that was making her so unhappy.

"She left shortly after you all arrived back from the hearing," the man said, as he took Grayson's gloves and hat. "She said there was a note for you on your desk in the library."

Grayson strode down the corridor, a sinking feeling in his stomach. There was no reason for Addie to have left for Bath before the rest of them.

The note was in a cream-colored envelope propped up against the lamp on the desk. With shaky hands, he picked up the envelope and slid the folded paper out. Taking a deep breath, he read:

*Dear Grayson,*
*I haev returned to Bath. To my own huose. We do not nede to*
*remain togethr. This was obbviousle a misteke.*
*Yours,*
*Addie*

THE PAPER FLOATED TO THE FLOOR AS HE DROPPED HIS HEAD IN his hands. This was the first time he'd seen a note written by his wife. He smiled at the misspellings caused by the word blindness, or rather dyslexia, she suffered from. Then he realized how very difficult her life had been because of it.

She was a courageous woman. She left the comfort of her parent's home, struck out on her own, and made her business a success. No wonder she resented him dismissing it so easily.

He'd been an arse. There was nothing else to be said for it. He needed to go after her and tell her how proud he was of her and how much he loved her, would always love her.

She was his other half. The warmth to his coldness, the last piece of the puzzle that put his heart back together. She was a great mother, a wonderful friend, kind and gracious, and the most important person in the world to him.

*No, my love, our marriage was not a mistake. We belong to each other and will always until the day we die.*

Grayson walked to the end of the corridor and shouted, "Brooks, get that carriage ready to take me to the train station."

The man beamed bright enough to light up the cloudiest day in London. "Yes, my lord. Right away, my lord."

Grayson bounded up the stairs, determination in every step. He would get his wife back and never let her go. The two of them and Michael would be a real family. And more children would follow. Lots of them. A nursery full of them.

He threw a few items in a satchel and crossed the corridor

from his room and entered Michael's room. Mrs. Banfield was sitting with him at a small table, both of them sharing tea.

"Mrs. Banfield. It has come to my attention that I must leave for Bath this afternoon. Please continue with the original plans we made to return tomorrow. I purchased the tickets today and will leave them, along with money for your trip, on the desk in my library."

"Yes, my lord." The woman must have known something was in the air by the bright smile on her face, too. He'd begun to feel that everyone surrounding him knew he loved Addie, but he hadn't made sure she knew it. They were correct, and he was on a mission to straighten all of that out.

He squatted in front of Michael. Using the little bit of sign language he remembered, he told Michael he was returning to Bath and that he and Mrs. Banfield would join him the next day.

The boy smiled and signed back that he loved him, and loved his new mama, too.

Right. That was what this was all about. He loved Michael's new mama, too, and it was time and past that he told her so.

He accepted Michael's hug and left the room, racing down the stairs. "Is my carriage ready?"

"Yes, my lord." Brooks handed him a piece of paper. "Here is the train schedule. You have three more trains leaving today."

"Good." He shrugged into his coat, accepted his hat and gloves from his butler, and left the house, whistling all the way down the stairs to the carriage.

A man on a mission.

## 15

THE EARLY MORNING SUN WARMED HER BACK AS ADDIE INSERTED the key into the lock of Once Upon a Book. It was well over two hours before the store was due to open, but since she'd tossed and turned all night, there didn't seem to be any reason to remain in bed to further torture herself.

The familiar scent of books, glue, ink, and paper rolled over her as she stepped over the threshold. She took a deep breath, but the warm, tingly feeling of happiness and a sense of accomplishment that she always felt when she walked into her store was missing.

She was just tired, she told herself. That was the only reason her normal reaction was absent. Her bookstore always gave her a feeling of satisfaction.

Except now it didn't.

She glanced at the front window where she would work on her Christmas display. The excitement wasn't there. All she felt was worn out.

And alone.

And miserable.

This was absolute nonsense, she scolded herself. The fact that she left her store in the care of her friends to accompany

Grayson and his son to help select a tutor for the boy, and ended up married, was irrelevant. She had wanted to have her own bookstore for years.

She had managed to get it and prosper. She would love it again. As much as she loved . . .

Stop.

Turning in a circle, she breathed in deeply. Life had taken an unexpected turn, but there was no reason why she could not resume her old life and be quite happy with it. One did certainly not need a husband to enjoy life. Hadn't that been what she and Pamela and Lottie had promised themselves? And each other?

In an effort to convince herself, she walked toward a pile of books in the corner that needed her attention. Whoever had been minding the store in her absence when the packages had arrived had placed them there. The collection of boxes was most likely her Christmas order.

She stopped in front of the neatly stacked pile and stared at it. Where was the thrill, the happiness at preparing for her first Christmas as the owner of a bookstore? Why did everything seem so blasted wearisome?

With a deep sigh, she bent over the pile and began to sort them out. At least she had gotten her large order of *A Christmas Carol*. They would sell well. In her meanderings, she never heard the door open behind her.

"I love this sight as much as I did the first time I walked into this store." Grayson's deep voice startled her. The rush of excitement that had been missing when she entered her store returned.

Slowly she stood and faced him, her heart pounding in her chest. "What are you doing here?"

Goodness, in the mere hours they'd been apart, she'd forgotten how handsome he was. How his soft, crooked smile did strange things to her insides, and the few strands of his hair that always fell onto his forehead made her want to push them back.

He was dressed in his normal attire of well-fitting gray trousers, a crisp white shirt, charcoal waistcoat, fashionably tied ascot, and black wool jacket that hugged his broad shoulders.

He shrugged. "I decided to return last evening instead of this morning." For the first time, she noticed the strain on his face. A sense of wariness.

Addie patted her hair and took a deep breath. "I see."

Well, that was certainly very loquacious of her. She'd never had a problem speaking before, but it seemed her normal ability to converse had escaped her.

She tried again. "Why are you here in my store?" There. That was a full sentence. She knew she could do it.

"Because my wife is here." He placed his hands on his hips as he regarded her.

She snorted. Lack of words again.

He grinned. "Are you not Lady Adeline Berkshire, my wife?"

She refused to be addled. Or at least anymore addled than she was right now with her husband standing a mere two feet from her when he was supposed to be in London. "My lord—"

"Grayson."

"I thought the note I left you was quite sufficient to explain how things are going to be."

When he grinned even wider, his eyes twinkling with humor, she closed her eyes and sighed. "The note was a mess, wasn't it?"

When she looked back at him, he had moved closer. The familiar scent of bergamot combined with the heat emanating from his body overwhelmed her. She attempted to back up, but the pile of books was behind her, and if she continued, she would fall on her bottom.

He grabbed her by her arms, most likely seeing the danger

she was in of landing in a heap. "Perhaps there was a misspelling here and there, but I got the general idea. However, I fail to see why you believe our marriage was a mistake." He actually looked confused, which raised her ire.

As usual, when she was angry, she didn't stop to think. "It is hard to be in a marriage when one's husband is still in love with his deceased wife." She slapped her hand over her mouth, wishing with all her might that she could bring the words back.

Grayson released her arms and shook his head as if to clear his thoughts. "What?"

Addie managed to slip by him, feeling much more in control with him not quite so close. "Mrs. Hartley visited one day."

"Ah." He nodded.

"She told me that your heart had been broken when your wife died, and you were adamant that you would never marry again. You loved Margaret with your whole heart, and no one could ever take her place."

Grayson wavered between wanting to pull Addie into his arms and kiss her senseless, or seeking out his nasty, mean sister-in-law and threatening her with cutting off her funds.

He had foolishly felt guilty when Peter had died and left his wife with nothing but bills. Grayson paid off her debts and set up a monthly allowance for her and her son. His solicitor had suggested cutting her off when she first filed the lawsuit against Michael, but he could not allow the woman and her son to starve.

Considering the pain she'd caused his wife, he could now, however.

"Addie, I won't say you misunderstood because I am quite certain Beatrice wanted you to think precisely what you did.

However, the love I felt for my wife when she died had long since faded into nothingness."

"Why?"

Grayson ran his fingers through his hair. "Margaret was not a nice person. I didn't see her true character until the year of our marriage. She was self-centered, vain, a very poor mother, and was having an affair with my brother."

He moved close to her again and took her hands in his. "When I told Beatrice that I would never marry again, it was because I didn't trust myself not to fall in love with someone who would then break my heart."

Addie tilted her head and frowned. "I don't understand."

"Understand this. I love you, Addie. Not with the lust-filled fancy of youth, but with a mature, all-encompassing love that will last a lifetime. One that is deeper, more intense than anything I have ever known." He kissed her knuckles. "I want you by my side for the rest of my life. I want to have children, lots of children that we can spoil and brag about to our friends. And I can only hope that if you agree to continue our marriage that one day you might feel the same about me."

His stomach dropped when she shook her head. Then she looked up at him with tears brimming in her eyes. "I already love you that way, Grayson. I was terrified when Mrs. Hartley came to call and said those words. All my dreams of a happy married life vanished."

Not able to stand it any longer, Grayson pulled her into his arms. "No, my love. We shall have the best of marriages. Our friends will envy us and avoid being in our company because we will be so besotted with each other."

Addie started laughing, which in turn had him laughing as well. "We will have to live an isolated life. No friends."

"With all those children?" she asked.

"Yes. Many children. Ah, Addie. I love you so much." He finally kissed her the way he wanted to kiss her. Just as he was settling in for a long session of kissing and possibly a bit more if he locked the door, Addie placed her hands between them and shoved him away.

"What?" He reached for her to pull her back.

Addie stepped back and crossed her arms under her lovely breasts, making it difficult to concentrate on what she was saying.

"What about my store?"

"Your store?" He loved how her lips had already plumped up from his kiss. He quickly glanced at the door and figured it would only take a few seconds to skirt around her and lock it.

"Yes. You intend to sell my store."

Anxious to get to the next step, Grayson waved her off. "You may keep the store. Run it. Sell it. Burn it down. I don't care. It's yours to do with as you please." He reached out to pull her back to him.

"Wait!" She put her hand up. "Do you mean that?" She smirked. "Or are you just saying that so you can lock the front door you've been eyeing for the past few minutes?"

He shook his head. "No. I'm serious, Addie. It was quite obnoxious of me to assume that you would want to give up what you built because you married me. If you wish to continue running the bookstore, then I will have the only countess in Bath who earns her own money."

Addie stepped into his arms. "Truthfully, I found when I entered the store today that the same thrill was not there."

Grayson kissed her on her nose. "I will leave that decision entirely up to you." He eyed the door once more. "May I lock the door now?"

She sighed and rested her head on his chest. "Yes, please."

The bookstore, Once Upon a Book, on the corner of George Street and Broad Street, in Bath, England, remained closed for the rest of that day.

# EPILOGUE

*Four months later*

ADDIE SAT BACK ON HER HEELS AFTER HAVING EMPTIED HER stomach into the chamber pot she kept handy since she didn't always make it to the water closet in time.

"Feel better, sweetheart?" Grayson sat alongside her, rubbing her back. He handed her a glass of water that she used to rinse her mouth out.

"Yes. And in a few minutes, I will be hungry again." She moved to stand up, but Grayson rose before her and reached out to help her up.

He wrapped her in his arms and pulled her close. "Dr. Hatfield told me this stomach problem will diminish as your pregnancy progresses."

Addie shook her head. "You're not supposed to say that word."

He leaned back to look at her. "Nonsense. All this silliness about not saying 'leg' or 'pregnant' or 'menstruation' is ridiculous."

"Well, at least not in public, if you please."

Grayson bent and scooped her into his arms. He carried her to the large bed in the center of the room and laid her on the colorful counterpane and sat alongside her. "You should rest."

Addie raised herself up on her elbows. "All I've been doing is resting. I do three things: rest, eat, throw up, and sleep. Sorry, that's four things." She dropped back on the pillow.

"Makes for a busy day." He smoothed the hair back that had fallen onto her forehead while she was hanging over the chamber pot.

"My lady, Miss Danvers has called. Are you receiving?" Sybil stood at the entrance to Addie's bedchamber.

How odd. She, Lottie, and Pamela would be meeting for tea in a few hours. Since Addie was no longer running the store, they had moved their daily meeting from Once Upon a Book to the Berkshire townhouse since it was the roomiest residence of the three women.

"Yes. Of course. Tell her I will be right down." She swung her legs over the edge of the bed and gripped the coverlet with both hands as a wave of dizziness washed over her.

"I don't think you should be receiving anyone today, my love." Grayson eyed her with concern. "Why not ask her to join you up here? Lottie is certainly a close enough friend."

Addie nodded. "Yes. That is a good idea. Will you please go downstairs and have her come up?"

Her husband leaned over and kiss her on the lips. "I will also send up some tea and toast."

"Yes. Thank you."

Grayson had been quite solicitous since she'd announced being in a family way. Based on the counting she'd done, she was about three months along, which made the baby due in October. Precisely a year from when the impatient Lord Berkshire had first walked into her store.

She had worked in her bookstore through the Christmas

season, but with trying to do things for her family, keeping up with Michael's sign language, and hiring additional staff to keep the townhouse in Bath running smoothly, she was only too happy to see the beginning of the new year.

Things went smoothly until mid-February when the fatigue returned, and Grayson insisted she visit with Dr. Hatfield, who confirmed she was expecting.

With her morning sickness and her need for at least one nap each day, she had to hire someone to look after the store. However, the more she thought about it, the more she considered perhaps selling the store was the best thing for her to do.

Since it was now her decision instead of Grayson's, it didn't seem so terrible. She had Michael to care for and in several months a new baby. Grayson had contracted for the building of another house further outside of Bath to accommodate his burgeoning family, which would also include her parents, who had announced they would be moving to Bath.

Grayson had insisted her parents live with them until they could find a house they wanted. Mother was thrilled and excited that she would reside with her daughter and her children. Amazingly enough, Addie was happy to have her mother close at a time like this.

That would require decorating and furnishing and adding even more staff. As much as she loved her store, she'd begun to believe it was truly time to move fully into her new life.

A light tap on her door drew her attention. "Come in."

Lottie entered the room, her beautiful face blotchy from crying. She twisted a handkerchief in her hands.

Addie reached out to her. "What's wrong, Lottie?"

Her friend took in a shuddering breath. "I have to leave Bath."

Addie was stunned. "Leave Bath! Why?" She patted the space alongside her.

Lottie sat and dabbed at her eyes with her handkerchief.

"Because I just came from Milsom Street, where I was taking tea with one of my students." Another deep breath. "Lord Sterling walked into the shop and greeted me."

Addie waited patiently for Lottie to pull herself together. "Yes?"

"Don't you see? I can't stay in Bath. Lord Sterling has moved here permanently." Her agitation was contagious. Addie's heartbeat sped up, and she felt a growing sense of doom.

Trying her best to remain calm since getting upset with Lottie in the state she was in would not help, she said softly, "And?"

"He knows my mother. Everyone in London knows my mother. Now everyone in Bath will as well. I must leave." She hopped up to escape, and Addie grabbed her skirt. "Wait. I don't understand."

Lottie attempted to pull away, but Addie held firm. "You came to tell me you have to leave Bath. I will not let you go until you explain why. And not just because he knows your mother."

She had no idea what Lottie would say, but she knew it was not going to be good news. Lottie covered her eyes with her hands. "My mother is Mrs. Danforth."

Stunned silence followed the words echoing around the room. Addie sucked in a deep breath. "Oh, no." She knew all about Mrs. Danforth. Even among young girls making their debuts, who should never know about such things, Mrs. Danforth was well-known. No wonder Lottie had never told her and Pamela why she had broken from her mother.

"Oh, yes." Lottie said. "The most expensive and notorious courtesan in London is my mama."

### The End

Did you like this story? Please consider leaving a review on either Goodreads or the place where you bought it. Long or short, your review will help other readers discover new authors and make purchasing decisions!

I hope you had fun reading Addie and Grayson's love story. Coming next in The Misfits of Bath series: *The Courtesan's Daughter and the Gentleman.*

Miss Charlotte Danvers has just received the biggest shock of her life. After spending most of her life in France in an elite school for girls, first as a student, and then as a teacher, she decides to return to London and take up residence with her mother.

When she arrives at her mother's townhouse in London, she is stunned to discover that the woman who raised her is a well-known courtesan.

After an angry and tearful confrontation with her mother, Charlotte leaves London and makes her home in Bath. All goes well until she meets Mr. Carter Westbrooke, close friend and business partner of Charlotte's best friend's husband, Lord Berkshire.

After only a few weeks, Mr. Westbrooke declares his intentions to Charlotte to make her his wife.

She can be no one's wife but cannot bring herself to tell him why. Must she run again?

*Get your copy on Amazon.*

You can find a list of all my books here: http://calliehutton.com/books/

# ABOUT THE AUTHOR

Callie Hutton, the *USA Today* bestselling author of *The Elusive Wife*, writes both Western Historical and Regency romance, with "historic elements and sensory details" (*The Romance Reviews*). She also pens an occasional contemporary or two. Callie lives in Oklahoma with several rescue dogs and her top cheerleader husband of many years. Her family also includes her daughter, son, daughter-in-law and twin grandsons affectionately known as "The Twinadoes."

Callie loves to hear from readers. Contact her directly at calliehutton11@gmail.com or find her online at www.calliehutton.com. Sign up for her newsletter to receive information on new releases, appearances, contests and exclusive subscriber content. Visit her on Facebook, Twitter and Goodreads.

Callie Hutton has written more than thirty books. For a complete listing, go to www.calliehutton.com/books

**Praise for books by Callie Hutton**

*A Wife by Christmas*

"A *Wife by Christmas* is the reason why we read romance...the perfect story for any season." --The Romance Reviews Top Pick

*The Elusive Wife*

"I loved this book and you will too. Jason is a hottie & Oliva is the kind of woman we'd all want as a friend. Read it!" --Cocktails and Books

"In my experience I've had a few hits but more misses with historical romance so I was really pleasantly surprised to be hooked from the start by obviously good writing." --Book Chick City

"The historic elements and sensory details of each scene make the story come to life, and certainly helps immerse the reader in the world that Olivia and Jason share." --The Romance Reviews

"You will not want to miss *The Elusive Wife*." --My Book Addiction

"...it was a well written plot and the characters were likeable." --Night Owl Reviews

*A Run for Love*

"An exciting, heart-warming Western love story!" --*NY Times* bestselling author Georgina Gentry

"I loved this book!!! I read the BEST historical romance last night...It's called *A Run For Love*." --*NY Times* bestselling author Sharon Sala

"This is my first Callie Hutton story, but it certainly won't be my last." --The Romance Reviews

*A Prescription for Love*

"There was love, romance, angst, some darkness, laughter, hope and despair." --RomCon

"I laughed out loud at some of the dialogue and situations. I think you will enjoy this story by Callie Hutton." --Night Owl Reviews

*An Angel in the Mail*

"...a warm fuzzy sensuous read. I didn't put it down until I was done." --Sizzling Hot Reviews

Visit http://calliehutton.com/ for more information.

Made in United States
North Haven, CT
24 October 2023

43159216R00107